SOLDIER BOYS

ALSO BY DEAN HUGHES

Four-Four-Two
Missing in Action
Search and Destroy

SOLDIER BOYS

DEAN HUGHES

ATHENEUM BOOKS FOR YOUNG READERS
New York London Toronto Sydney New Delhi

ATHENEUM BOOKS FOR YOUNG READERS

An imprint of Simon & Schuster Children's Publishing Division

1230 Avenue of the Americas, New York, New York 10020

For information about special discounts for bulk purchases, please contact Simon & Schuster Special Sales at 1-866-506-1949 or business@simonandschuster.com.

The Simon & Schuster Speakers Bureau can bring authors to your live event. For more information or to book an event, contact the Simon & Schuster Speakers Bureau at 1-866-248-3049 or visit our website at www.simonspeakers.com.

Also available in an Atheneum Books for Young Readers hardcover edition.

Interior design by Mike Rosamilia, cover design by Russell Gordon

The text for this book is set in Meridien LT Std.

Manufactured in the United States of America

First Atheneum Books for Young Readers paperback edition July 2015

10 9 8 7 6 5 4 3

The Library of Congress has cataloged the hardcover edition as follows:

Hughes, Dean 1943–

Soldier boys / Dean Hughes.

p. cm.

Summary: Two boys, one German and one American, are eager to join their respective armies during World War II, and their paths cross at the Battle of the Bulge.

ISBN 978-0-689-81748-9 (hc)

1. World War, 1939-1945—Juvenile fiction. [I. World War, 1939–1945—Fiction. 2. Ardennes, Battle of the, 1944–1945—Fiction. 3. Conduct of life—Fiction. 4. Soldiers—Fiction.] I. Title.

PZ7.H87312 So 2001

[Fic]—dc21

00-046920

ISBN 978-1-4814-2704-3 (pbk)

ISBN 978-1-4391-3214-2 (eBook)

FOR MY UNCLE, GARTH PIERCE,
WHO, WHEN A BOY HIMSELF, FOUGHT
IN THE BATTLE OF THE BULGE

ACKNOWLEDGMENTS

I have spent the last seven years doing research on World War II. I have studied hundreds of books and oral histories, have studied the newspapers of the era, and have done interviews with war veterans. All of this research has contributed to my knowledge of the era. Especially helpful to me for this novel were the following: *Citizen Soldiers: The U. S. Army from the Normandy Beaches to the Bulge to the Surrender of Germany* (Simon & Schuster, 1998) and *Band of Brothers: E Company, 506th Regiment, 101st Airborne from Normandy to Hitler's Eagle's Nest* (Simon & Schuster, 1992), both by Stephen E. Ambrose; *The Burden of Hitler's Legacy* (Renaissance House Publishers, 1988) by Alfons Heck; *Hitler's Last Gamble: The Battle of the Bulge* (HarperCollins, 1994) by Trevor N. Dupuy; *The Making of a Paratrooper: Airborne Training and Combat in World War II* (University Press of Kansas, 1990) by Kurt Gabel; *Doing Battle: The Making of a Skeptic* (Little, Brown and Co., 1996) and *Wartime: Understanding and Behavior in the Second World War* (Oxford University Press, 1989), both by Paul Fussell.

SOLDIER BOYS

CHAPTER I

Dieter watched the older boys dive into the pond, fearless. They plunged deep into the bright water, and then, after a frightening delay, erupted to the surface, their muscles shining, skin red. Dieter wished he were so bold and powerful. He wished he had men's hair on his body, that his voice rumbled. But he was ten, and these boys were all at least fourteen. They were in the *HJ*—the Hitler Youth—and he was still too young, only a member of the German "Young People"—the *Jungvolk.*

"Come on, babies," Hans Keller called. "Are you afraid to jump in?" He was seventeen and *Scharführer*—leader of the local troop. Dieter always wilted when he faced this giant of a boy. Hans was what Dieter wanted to be: manly, funny when he chose to be, and fierce when he commanded. Dieter loved Hans, always tried to be near him, and yet he feared him more than anyone he knew. "Strip down and cool off, little boys. This is your only chance, and then it's back to marching."

But none of the younger boys reacted. Dieter was troubled by the deep water, ashamed for the grown boys to see him naked.

"What are you scared of, *children*? The fish won't bite those little worms you hide in your pants."

The younger boys laughed, and they glanced around to see who would strip down. Then Willi Hofmann dropped to the ground and began unlacing his boots. He was twelve but not much bigger than Dieter. "I'm not afraid to do it," Willi said. "Come on, Dieter, go with me."

Dieter breathed deep, tried to think what he would do.

"Deeee-ter," Willi pleaded, stretching the sound of his nickname, shortened from Dietrich. "You must."

Dieter glanced at Hans Keller, who was looking down, his hands on his naked hips, his feet set wide apart. Dieter had to show Hans that he could do this. He sat down too, and pulled at his shoestring. But he didn't hurry.

By the time Dieter had pulled off his boots, Willi had taken off his uniform shirt, dropped his short pants in the dirt, and his underpants, and then, with his white bottom glowing, had run away from Dieter and leaped into the water, feetfirst. He hit the water, hardly penetrated, and popped up quickly. He squealed at the cold, and laughed. The older boys laughed too, in those deep voices, and Dieter knew he had to do this. But he could hear his heart, the rush of blood in his ears. He stood up, pulled off his clothes, and didn't hesitate. He ran and jumped, as Willi had done, felt the hard surface slap his hip, and then he flailed at the water, desperate to stay on top. He paddled for the bank, his breath gone, the cold stabbing like thistles.

He was back on solid ground in only a few seconds, his body shivering. He ran to his clothes and began pulling his underwear back on, soaking them.

"Hey, what's the matter, Hedrick?" Hans yelled to Dieter. "You didn't stay in long enough to get used to the water. Look at Hofmann. He's still out there."

Most of the younger boys were hesitating—undressing slowly or staying back. But Dieter knew he hadn't done enough. It was Willi who was distinguishing himself, impressing the *Scharführer*. Dieter tossed his shirt back on the ground and pulled off his underwear. He walked back to the water, found what footing he could in the mud of the sloping bank, and forced himself forward until the water was up to his waist. Then he bent his knees and dropped into the painful cold. He looked up at Hans, naked and glistening, and waited for some sort of approval, but Hans was making fun of the other boys now, the little ones afraid to go in. "What would the *Führer* think of such girls as you?" he asked. "How can you grow up to be fighting men if you're scared of a little water?"

Dieter stayed down, forcing himself, but that wasn't

enough. He needed to swim about, like Willi, and show Hans that he wasn't afraid. And so he paddled into deeper water a few yards, then twisted and thrashed until he made it back to the bank, where he could get his feet into the mud and hold himself up. He waited and breathed a moment, and then he made another wild rush into the deeper water, and when he did, he heard what he had hoped for.

"Hey, you little boobs, look at Hedrick. He's only ten, and he's out there swimming like a man. What's wrong with the rest of you?"

That night, when Dieter lay in his warm feather bed, he thought of the cold water, and he thought of the way Hans had praised him in front of all the boys.

And after the swim, when the boys had dressed again, and hiked another hour, he remembered the speech that Hans had given. "If I push you boys," he told them, "it's because I must. We are at war now. Our Fatherland is threatened. We must all be men, not children; we must be ready to protect our mothers and sisters. We must stand with our *Führer* against the Polish aggressors."

Germany *was* at war. The week before, on September 1, 1939, German troops had marched into Poland and unleashed Hitler's new brand of warfare: *blitzkrieg*—lightning war. Troops and tanks and airplanes had all attacked in unison, and Polish troops were tumbling back like debris in a hurricane. Dieter's father claimed that in another few days, at the rate the German troops were moving, and with the Russians now attacking from the east, Poland would fall. Dieter listened with his father to the radio news every night, and the announcers spoke of nothing but great German victories. Dieter had also heard Hitler's fine speech to his people. Germany didn't want war, he said, but Poland had provoked this battle, and now the German army—the *Wehrmacht*—would show its valor.

Dieter thrilled to the words, hoping that the day would come when he could prove himself the way these valiant soldiers were doing. But Dieter's father was not as impressed. "I fear what might come next," he kept saying. "France and England won't be knocked about as easily as these Poles. This could be like the Great War. The fighting could go on for years."

Dieter knew all about the last war. Hans Keller, at the weekly *Jungvolk* meeting, had taught the boys what the thieving French and English had done. After the war, they had stolen land from Germany, forced Germans to pay the expenses of the war, and had kept the German people in poverty. Those same countries had also taken away Germany's military force, and with it, its pride, but the *Führer*, Adolf Hitler, had put a stop to that. Finally, someone was standing up for the Fatherland, making it a great nation again.

Dieter only wished that his father could understand what Hitler was doing for Germany—instead of talking weakness all the time. He had seen the worry and fear in his father's face, and in his mother's, and he was ashamed of them. Dieter's father had fought in the Great War as a young man, but he never spoke of the brave German boys who had given their lives. If he spoke of battle at all, he only whined about the mud and the trenches and the poor food—and his good fortune in surviving when so many had died. Dieter didn't like to think that his own father had been a coward, but it was hard to draw another conclusion. After the war, Father had come home to the town of Krumbach, in Bavaria, where he had taken over his family farm, and then he had married. Since then, he had done nothing important, and hardly ever left the farm.

Father was also such a quiet man, and small, with a voice too delicate. "We could be glad we have the farm before all this is over," he told Mother at breakfast one morning. "Last time, you know how it was, with never enough to eat."

"Could the war come here, Papa?" Elsa, Dieter's oldest sister, had asked.

"No, no. I doubt that," Father had told her. But his voice had sounded so timid that Dieter had had to stop eating and retreat from the kitchen. How could he think only of safety, of food, when Hitler was trying to raise up the German people?

"We are a peaceful people," Hans Keller had told the boys. "We don't want war. But if other countries want to fight, we won't turn our backs and run. We'll defend our Fatherland with all our strength. We'll *die* on the battle-field, if we must."

Dieter could hardly breathe.

"I won't be leading you much longer. I'll be joining the battle just as soon as I can. But know this: I am not afraid of death. I will make that sacrifice for my people. Now it is time for you to ask yourselves what you are will-ing to do. Will you die for Germany? Can you also make that promise?"

Hans was standing on a rock wall, his fists against his hips, magnificent as a statue, and he seemed to be staring directly at Dieter. *"Ja!"* Dieter had said, and the word had come out louder than he had intended. All the boys looked at him, and Hans had given Dieter a solemn nod. It was the best moment of his life, Dieter thought, the proudest. Now, Dieter's greatest worry was that the war would end too soon, and there would be no battles for him, that he would never have his chance to show he had meant what he had said.

Dieter had been with his family in Munich once, and he had seen the *Wehrmacht* on parade—all the grand tanks, the troop trucks, the artillery, the fighters flying overhead. And he had seen Adolf Hitler himself—his face stern. The soldiers in the parade had been like Hans Keller: disciplined, firm. Dieter had known then that this was the kind of man he wanted to be. Willi Hofmann was a good swimmer, but he was not serious. It was Dieter who would distinguish himself among the boys in his troop, and he would bring pride to his family. If he ever got a chance to go to war, he would return with medals, not with whining complaints. Or perhaps he would not return, but in Krumbach everyone would know of his bravery.

CHAPTER 2

Spencer Morgan was nervous. Almost scared.
He'd felt that way all Sunday afternoon, and again when he had gotten up that morning. And Mrs. Jorgensen, his tenth-grade English teacher, was only making things worse. She was a strict teacher, mean as a badger most of the time, but this morning she was fussing and crying about the war breaking out. Dad had said that the Japanese wouldn't try to drop bombs on Brigham City, and Spence told himself that was right. Utah was too far inland for that. But it wasn't bombs that worried him. He just felt shaky inside. Everything was going to change now—all at once. For one thing, his brother Robert was saying that he might go off and join the navy.

"I'm sure the president will declare war on Japan today," Mrs. Jorgensen told the students. "But there's no question we'll have to fight Germany, too. Germany has a treaty with Japan. Evil people always find each other; you can count on that. We'll be fighting Germans and Japs at the same time. And I just hope it won't last so long that some of you boys will have to get in on it."

Spence had turned fifteen a couple of weeks before, in November of 1941. He wondered, would this war really last that long? He didn't know. But everything was different today. It was like his life had picked up and moved over about a hundred miles, and nothing in front of him looked quite the same. He had come home from church the day before, gotten tired of waiting around for Sunday dinner, put on his old corduroys, and gone outside in the cold to throw a football around with his little brother, Lloyd. And then his big sister, Louise, had run outside and yelled, "The Japs are bombing Pearl Harbor. There's going to be a war."

Spence didn't know what Pearl Harbor was, but his sister made it sound like it was out in the Great Salt Lake, just a couple of miles away. But she was always like that. "Come on. Throw me the ball," Spence had told Lloyd, but Lloyd wanted to go in and listen to the radio.

So Spence had walked inside, and he had seen his mom and dad standing in front of their old Philco radio. His first thought had been that Sunday dinner was probably going to be slow in coming. And then he had heard the announcer's voice and seen the look on his father's face. That's when he had known this was serious. His mom was crying already, and she tried to hug him, but Spence wouldn't let her do that. He just listened. "World War," the announcer kept saying. It would be a world war. And America had lost most of its ships at Pearl Harbor—which was a place in the Hawaiian Islands.

"We could be in big trouble," Dad had whispered. That's when Spence noticed that his own hands were shaking.

"I'm signing up," Robert told his family when they had finally sat down to dinner. He was nineteen, almost twenty, and he worked in town, but he still lived at home. He had gone to Box Elder High School for a while but had quit during his junior year. Dad hadn't liked that, and said he shouldn't quit, but Robert had found a job at the flour mill, and jobs weren't easy to come by.

"Don't make up your mind about joining up just yet," Dad kept telling Robert, and finally he said why. "The bishop has you in mind to serve a mission. You know that. Just see how everything looks in a week or two, before you do anything too quick. I want you out preaching the gospel, not shooting at people."

The Morgans were Mormons, and Dad had served as a missionary for three years when he was a young man. He had gone to New Zealand to teach the Maori people, and he had never stopped telling stories about that. He had always said he wanted at least one of his sons to serve the same way, and Spence had figured that would be Robert. Spence himself didn't want to go off some-place far away—especially to preach. He was willing to go to church with his family, but he didn't much like reading the Bible or the Book of Mormon, and he sure didn't like preaching.

"We've worked too hard to save for your mission just to let it drop all at once," Dad told Robert.

The Morgan family ran an orchard outside Brigham, raised peaches and cherries and apricots, and Dad also did some carpenter work. He had been saving up all he could so that Robert could accept that mission call.

"Right now we've got to stop these Japs," Robert told his dad. "That's more important than anything. There won't be no use to preach anything if Hitler and the Japs—people like that—are running the world."

"Just hold your horses," Dad said. "You're not signing up until we have a good look at everything. Not every young man needs to go in, right off. Different boys have different priorities—and you've got the most important one of all."

But later, up in their bedroom—where Robert and Lloyd and Spence all slept—Robert had told the younger boys, "I don't need Dad's signature. I'm old enough. I can go sign up for myself."

"Yeah, and get yourself killed," Lloyd had said.

"You don't get it," Robert told him. "If a guy's a man, he has to do something. The Japs tricked us. They attacked our country and killed our boys. Now I've gotta kill some of them. Maybe that's not missionary work, but it's what's got to be done."

Now, at school, Spence kept thinking about all that. The Japs deserved what they got; that was for sure. But Robert wasn't much in a fight. He was big enough, had some arms and shoulders on him from bucking flour sacks, but everybody always said how nice he was. He never had been one to argue much, let alone get in a fist-fight. Maybe in the navy he wouldn't really have to shoot anyone and no one could shoot at him. But ships could sink. That's what Spence kept thinking about.

After Mrs. Jorgensen fussed and cried, she said she had to go down the hall for a minute to compose herself. "Please, just take out your copies of *Ivanhoe* and read silently," she said. "I won't be long." Then she stuck her nose in a handkerchief and hurried out the door.

LuAnn Crowther sat next to Spence. All fall he'd been trying to think of something to say to her, but he never had. Once in a while, she'd say, "The wind sure blew hard last night," or something like that, and Spence would say, "It sure did," but he had always wanted to think of something else to say, maybe after class while they were walking out. Every time he almost did, though, he clammed up at the last minute. He never had been one to say very much.

Now, though, as soon as Mrs. Jorgensen was gone,

LuAnn said to Kathleen Richards, the girl in front of Spence, "I'm scared about all our boys going off to war."

And Spence took that chance to say, "My brother Robert is signing up."

LuAnn turned and looked at Spence with her brown eyes big and round as chocolate drops. The breath went out of him. Since fourth grade he had watched her, always thinking someday, when he was old enough, he would see if she would go with him to a dance or a show, but always just as sure that she would want to go with Elvin Batcheldor or someone like that. Elvin was taller than Spence, could play better at sports, and he had nice clothes to wear all the time.

"That makes me just sick to hear it," LuAnn said. "Robert's so handsome. What if he goes off and gets killed by the Japs?"

Spence thought for a time before he said, "I guess he can take care of himself."

LuAnn was nodding by then and saying, "I'm sorry, Spencer. I shouldn't have said that. I guess you've got enough to worry about without me popping off that way."

Spence, of course, had been worrying about Robert going off and never coming back—but he didn't think of that now. He thought of how strong in the shoulders Robert was, how tall, and LuAnn saying that he was handsome. Robert had dark hair, like Mom, and brown eyes. Girls always said how good-looking he was. But

Spence was like his dad, with buckskin-colored hair and no eyebrows to speak of, even freckles. His teeth had come in crooked, too. Not once in his whole life had any girl said he was handsome. But LuAnn was the girl every guy in the school talked about. She had dimples that popped in like little flashes, and teeth almost perfect.

Spence knew he had to say something. Now or never. "I'll sign up too," he told LuAnn, "just as soon as they'll let me."

LuAnn laughed, and he saw those dimples. "Hold on a minute, Spencer. I don't think they're looking for tenth-grade boys just yet."

Spence sat up straight. He thought of what his Dad had said, and Mrs. Jorgensen. "This war could go on a few years," he said. "I guess I'll be in it before it's over."

But LuAnn was smiling at him now. "Well, I hope you start to grow a little by then. Right now you'd be shorter than your rifle."

"I'll grow plenty."

"I suppose you will," she said, and she seemed to think so. Spence could feel he was turning red.

But Kathleen was laughing at him. "You'd better do your homework. That's what you'd better do," she said. "In the army they won't want to hear all those excuses you think up every day."

Spence didn't say anything about that. But, he told himself, someday he'd *show* what he could do. He'd grow a few inches taller by then, and he'd sign up, the very first chance he got. He'd been a little nervous about all the changes since yesterday, and about Robert going off, but that was all. He was no coward. LuAnn would know, when the time came, what kind of a man he could be.

CHAPTER 3

Robert waited a few weeks before his dad agreed, and then he signed up for the navy. The whole family had fussed about it, and Mom had cried a lot, but now, two years later, not much had happened to him. In all his letters he complained about being stuck in San Diego, working on ships, not going to sea.

By then, Spence figured he'd waited a long time for his turn, and he wasn't going to let the same thing happen to him. He had it all figured out how he could get into the paratroopers. The only trouble was, his dad didn't want him to sign up yet. "You can't join without my signature, not till you're eighteen," he told Spence, "and you're not even seventeen yet."

Spence didn't want to lose his temper. He took a breath, waited a few seconds, and said, "Dad, I'm close enough to seventeen to start my paperwork. That's what they told me at the recruiting office down in Ogden. But you're right. I do have to have your signature."

"I'm not signing, Spence. I want you to finish high school."

"I already quit. I turned in my books this afternoon."

It was early November 1943. Spence was standing in front of his dad, out in the barn. Dad had been leaning over the old International Harvester tractor he had managed to keep running for way too many years now. His hands were covered with grease, his overalls. There was even a smear across one lens of his little round eyeglasses. But behind those glasses, Dad's eyes were set like ball bearings.

Spence had seen this standoff coming. But he wasn't going to wait until he was eighteen. If he did, the war could be over.

Dad was still clinging to a wrench, but he stepped aside, set it on his workbench, and then wiped his hands on a dirty rag. "Listen, Spence, I'm glad you want to do your part. There's nothing wrong with that. But we have one son in the military, and that's enough for now. This war won't go away as fast as you think. And I need you around here. I could get you a deferment for farmwork, easy, even if you were eighteen."

It all sounded reasonable, and that's what bothered Spence. He wasn't going to be talked out of this. He had thought about it too long. "Dad, Robert's not in any kind of danger. So that's not a good reason."

"But what's the big rush?"

"Look, Dad, I'm flunking two of my classes. I'm not going to graduate, anyway. So I'm out of school either way."

"The only reason you're flunking classes is that you don't give school half a try. You're smarter than any of my kids. You just don't do your work." He leaned back against his bench and let out a long breath. "What you really need is to grow up. You're sixteen years old, and sometimes you don't even act *that* old."

"Maybe I don't. But if I need to grow up, maybe the army will show me how." It wasn't something Spence was sure he believed, but it was something to say—something Dad might listen to.

"Yes, and two days into basic training, you might figure you've already learned enough—and want out."

Spence shook his head. That wasn't fair. He could do hard things when he cared about them. He'd played hard at football practice and then spent the games sitting on the bench, and he hadn't complained about that. He hadn't quit, either. "Dad, I know guys who've forged their father's signature and gotten in that way. But I did this straight. I came to you. All I want to do is fight for my country. It seems like that ought to make you proud."

"I'm just not sure that's the whole story."

"What else is it, then?"

"I think you want to prove something to LuAnn Crowther."

"*No!* She's got nothing to do with this."

"Maybe. Maybe not. I'm not sure *you* know. As small as you are, you weren't cut out for football, but you always thought you had to show up that Stevens boy. Or try, anyway."

Spence held on, tried not to lose his temper, but he was gripping his induction papers tightly enough to make a mess of them. "This sure is something, Dad," he said, his voice tight. "Everywhere you look there's a sign saying how we ought to be loyal to the country—fight for it and everything. So I tell you that's what I want to do, and you tell me I'm a good-for-nothing." He held the papers up, close to his father's chin. "That ain't right, Dad. It's not fair. Lots of boys seventeen are going now, and they don't have to listen to all that."

"Yes, and a lot of those boys are getting themselves killed."

"So what do you want to do—keep me home and let some other man's son die?"

That stopped Dad. He looked down at the floor. After a time he said, "I'd feel better if I saw a little more religion in you, Spence, more like Robert. You don't know how soldiers live. When they go on leave, the first thing they do is head to some cathouse."

"Well, I won't. I can tell you that right now. And one thing I don't do is break promises."

"No, you don't. I'll say that."

Dad was staring into Spence's eyes, and Spence tried hard not to blink, not to look away. Finally, Dad's hand came out and took hold of the papers. "All right. Fine. I don't know what your mom's going to say. I'll try to explain it to her. But I'm telling you, if you come home cussing and drinking and smoking cigarettes, you'll break your mother's heart."

"I told you, I won't." He handed his father his fountain pen, and Dad spread the forms out across the fender of the old tractor—and he signed.

But Spence was still a little angry. Dad had had no right to make that crack about LuAnn. She had made her choice, and now he was making his. He was going to be a paratrooper. The year before, a boy Spence knew—Buddy Howard—had come home on furlough. The guy had been nothing special in high school, hadn't played football or anything like that, but he'd gone into the army and he'd made it into Airborne training. He was in the 101st Division and wore one of those Screaming Eagle patches on his shoulder and wings above his pocket. The Airborne guys tucked their pant legs inside their jump boots and then bloused them out. That's how you knew who they were. And no one messed with those boys. Everyone knew how tough they were.

Spence had never been up in an airplane in his life, but he had known when he'd listened to Buddy Howard that that's what he was going to do: wear his pants like that and jump out of airplanes. The recruiter had told Spence that he was a little small—but still, above the minimum size requirement. If he could pass the intelligence test to get in, he could go straight to Georgia, where the Airborne had a great program: basic training and jump school at the same time. All the training was doubled up, and hard, but a guy would be ready to get into the action quicker that way. Before long, American troops would be parachuting into Europe, and Spence would be in time to get in on that. That's exactly what he wanted: to see some real action, not some mop-up when the war was nearly over.

LuAnn was going steady with a boy named Dennis Stevens—the banker's son—and everyone said the two of them would get married as soon as she graduated. That was fine. Spence had gone with her some, the year before, but that was over now. She had her life, and he had his. He was going to be in the best military unit in all the services. Someday he'd come home on leave or something like that, and everyone in town would see what he had done.

Dad folded the papers and handed them back to Spence. Then he cupped his hand on top of Spence's shoulder. "Son, I *am* proud of you. But I gotta tell you, I feel a little sick inside. To me, you're still a boy. It seems like just a couple of days ago, you were trailing around here in a diaper—usually wet and dragging in the dirt, too."

Spence rolled his eyes, but he smiled. "Hey, I'm going to miss everybody myself, Dad. I know I will."

"No, I don't think you do know."

"Well, maybe not." It *was* strange to think of leaving home. He thought he would miss Lloyd, who was twelve now, the most, and his two younger sisters almost as much. Evelyn was nine, and Betty just six. Louise tried to boss him too much, but the little ones were funny and they liked him. He could always tell that they did.

Dad reached out his hand, and Spence did, too. They shook hands and nodded. "Son, I hope you'll turn to God for support. If you do, this experience could deepen your faith. Maybe that's what you need right now."

"Maybe I do, and maybe it will," Spence said, but he didn't want to get into all that, either. Dad could really get wound up when he started talking religion.

"I want you to make me another promise, too."

"What's that?"

"A young kid like you gets out there and doesn't know the ropes, the first thing he does, right off, is try to be a hero, and he gets himself shot up. If you go off and do that, I don't know how I'll even look at your mom. Will you use your head, and not take a lot of chances out there?"

"It'll be dangerous, Dad. A soldier can't—"

"I know all that. But you won't take extra chances, will you? You won't stick your neck out where you don't need to?"

"No, I won't, Dad. I won't be stupid."

* * *

Mom was upset that night—mad at first, and then all brokenhearted. Spence didn't know what to say to her. "I promised Dad about things I won't get into, Mom," he told her. "So you don't have to worry about that."

"You have no idea what you're getting into, Spencer. You're just a boy."

Spence got out of the house. He found his friend Earl Nilson, and they went down to the bowling alley and played some pool. Earl was jealous. He wouldn't be seventeen until February, and even then, he knew his parents would never sign. He told some of the guys around the bowling alley about Spence, and everyone had something to say to him. Spence didn't say anything about doing his part, nothing like that, but when Ty Groberg, a guy about forty or so, said, "You'll be missing your mama before long," Spence just said, "I guess I'll be all right."

The next morning Spence took the train—the Bamberger line—to Ogden, and he dropped off his induction papers. The recruiter promised to start things moving. "We can call you in, right as soon as you hit seventeen," he said, "but I can't guarantee nothing about any Airborne assignment unless you pass that test."

"Can I take it right now?" Spence asked.

"Sure. No problem. It takes a while, though."

"That's all right. I got time."

So Spence took the test, and felt like he did all right,

and then he caught the train back to Brigham City. And when he got off, he walked down Main Street, under the giant sycamore trees. The walks were littered with big brown leaves—and Spence thought of all the times he had strolled down this street in the fall, and the time he had marched in the Peach Days Parade with his junior high drum-and-bugle corps. He went straight to Dale's, a little malt and hamburger shop. A lot of kids went there after school; it was about time for them to start coming in.

Spence was eating a hamburger at the counter when LuAnn arrived. She worked there after school. She walked out from the kitchen and stopped long enough to tie on her apron before she said, "Hi, Spencer."

He nodded, but he didn't say anything yet.

Still, she walked down to him. "I heard you quit school."

He nodded again.

"Earl told me your dad signed your papers."

"He did."

"When do you go in?"

"On my birthday, or right around there."

"Twenty-fourth of November?"

Spence's head came up. He didn't think she would know that.

"What's your rush, Spencer?"

"If I'm going, anyway, there's no reason to wait around."

She looked worried a little, or maybe confused. Spence liked something about that. But he hated to look at her. As long as he could remember, he had known she was the prettiest girl he would ever see. And he had known, just as sure, that she would never feel anything for him. He had finally gotten up the nerve, the year before, to ask her to a dance, and then she had gone with him to the pictures and things like that all that winter, but eventually she had started making excuses, and her friend, Myrna Wagstaff, had told Spence, "It's nothing against you, Spence. She just likes Dennis Stevens a little better, I think."

Dennis was one of the rich boys in town. He wore argyle sweaters to school, and he took vacations with his family to California when no one else could come by enough gasoline to drive that far. He was president of the junior class, too. But he was stuck on himself worse than anyone Spence knew. LuAnn could have the guy, if that's who she wanted.

"What are you going into? Army or—"

"Paratroopers."

"Are those the ones who jump out of airplanes?"

"Sure they are."

She smiled, finally, and her dimples appeared. She had pretty hair, blond and a little red, and curly. And those brown eyes. "That'd scare me half to death."

Spence had tried a thousand times in the last year just to settle in and hate the girl. But there was nothing to hate. She was always nice to him—nice to everybody, really. And not conceited, either, like some pretty girls. The only thing wrong with LuAnn was that she had no more sense than to like Dennis Stevens.

"I want to see what it's like," Spence said. "There's nothing around here that's halfway as exciting as jumping out of an airplane."

"Well . . . be sure to come down soft."

And then she walked away, had to take care of a customer who had just sat down at the other end of the counter. Spence wanted to stay, but he had finished his hamburger, and there was no excuse to sit there. So he left half a dollar—which allowed for a fifteen-cent tip— on the counter and he walked outside. He could have used the phone inside and called his dad for a ride home, but the farm was only a couple of miles out of town, and he thought maybe he wanted to walk. It was cold out, a little windy, and he hadn't worn his winter coat, but as he walked, he warmed up.

He kept thinking about what LuAnn had said: "Come down soft." But he had heard the sympathy in her voice. She knew, the way girls always knew, that he was crazy about her—or had been once, anyway—and that made her pity him. It would always be that way, as long as he stayed around town. Maybe when he got back, she'd be married to Dennis, but at least she would see some medals on his chest, or read about him in the paper and know what he'd done in the war. Then she wouldn't feel sorry for him. And by then, he really wouldn't care anything at all about her. He'd finally be over all that, completely, and he'd find some other girl.

That night, after dinner, Spence read the *Ogden Standard-Examiner*, read all about the progress of the war. Marines were fighting in the Solomon Islands, in a place called Bougainville. Italy had surrendered that fall, but American and British troops were fighting Germans, north of Rome. And near Kiev, a bad battle was going on between the Germans and the Russians. Spence was interested in all that, but he was especially curious about predictions he kept seeing that another front of the war would be opened in Europe, probably in France, by the spring of 1944. That's the landing he wanted to be in on.

He was listening to band music on the radio and still looking through the paper when Louise came into the room. "Did you read the casualty list in the paper?" she asked.

"What?" Spence looked up. He could tell by her voice that she had something on her mind.

"Didn't you read the casualty list?"

"I glanced at it." Every day, in the paper, there was a list of Utahans killed, wounded, or missing in action. Some nights there were seven or eight on the list, and other nights, over twenty.

"Is that what you want—your name in the paper?"

Louise was a little older than Spence, nineteen, but sometimes she seemed to think she was his mother. She was a nice enough girl, in most ways, but she had an opinion about everything.

"Not for getting killed, if that's what you mean."

"I don't see why you're doing this. You could wait and go next year."

"I already talked to Dad about that. I don't need to explain it all to you."

But then he saw tears in her eyes. She was a pretty girl, in a way—at least for a big sister—but he hated seeing her like this, biting down on her lip, her chin beginning to shake.

"Nothing's going to happen to me, sis. So don't start all that."

"You don't know that."

That was true, but it wasn't something Spence worried much about.

"I don't think you can kill anyone either. You can't even spank Laddie when he doesn't mind you."

Laddie was the family's old collie.

"A man can do what he has to do—when the time comes."

"Oh, Spencer, don't try to sound like that. You're not a man yet and you know it. This whole thing just makes me sick. You're doing this to show up LuAnn—and she doesn't give a *hoot* about you."

"It's got nothing to do with her. I don't know why everybody thinks that."

"We know you, Spence. That's why. You're going to get into this war, right up to your neck, and then you're finally going to realize you've made a big mistake."

Spence didn't like that. She had no right to start talking that way. But after she was gone, he did think about killing. Sometimes he hunted jackrabbits with his friends, out north of the lake by Promontory Point. One thing he'd always hated was that squealing sound a rabbit made after it was shot—and the way it would flop all around. He didn't know what it might be like to shoot a man. But he told himself it didn't have to be something he liked to do, or even wanted to do. It was just one of those things that had to be done. It wasn't anything at all like spanking a dog he had practically grown up with. That had been a stupid thing for Louise to bring up.

CHAPTER 4

Spence was glad for the shower, for the short escape from the Georgia heat and humidity, but he didn't have the strength to get his clothes on, or to walk to the mess hall. He flopped down on his bunk with only a towel wrapped around him. He thought about staying right there, just going to sleep now, at six in the afternoon.

But then Ted Draney dropped onto the bunk next to Spence's. He let out a long moan and said, "Spence, I'm sorry, but I've made up my mind. I'm quitting."

Three days before, the two boys had met for the first time, but they were already old friends, it seemed to Spence, after what they had gone through together. They had ended up, just by accident, sitting next to each other on the bus that brought them to this ugly plot of ground the men called "the Frying Pan." It was Fort Benning, by Columbus, Georgia: a training ground for army infantrymen—and for paratroopers. Two big towers, 250 feet high, stood over the place like a couple of hangman's gallows. What the trainees all knew was that before they could jump from an airplane, they had to jump from one of those towers, and that seemed a lot more frightening. Ted, another Western boy, from Colorado, had looked out the bus window that first day and said, "Man, I don't know if I can do that—jump off there."

But Spence had told him, "Sure you can. We'll stick together and get through this place."

That had sounded good at the time, but now the only thing Spence could think was that Ted was right, that they both ought to quit. He had considered that option hundreds of times in the last three days, and sometimes it didn't seem so much a choice as a last hope—the only escape out of hell.

But that's not what he said. "I can't quit, Ted. I just can't. And you promised to stick it out with me."

Neither spoke for a time after that. They stayed stretched out on their backs, both of them taking long, slow breaths. This was spring. Everyone had told Spence he was lucky to be here now and not when it was so wickedly hot in the summer, but the humidity was still unbelievable, like nothing Spence had ever known at home. This ugly barracks—rough, like some new but shoddy barn inside—seemed to suck in the moisture and hold it. Spence felt like he was breathing in as much water as air. And part of that was that he had run—double time, they called it—almost all day for three days, and marched or done push-ups when he wasn't running. "Hit it for twenty-five," the drill sergeant would shout at any odd time. Always twenty-five. Sometimes, just as the men got back to their feet, he'd command them to hit it a second time. And then he'd get them up and running again.

"This is our last chance," Ted said. "You know what happens to us if we quit tomorrow."

"Ted, I can't. There's just no way I can do that."

The same little conversation had gone through his own mind over and over. He would decide to drop out, tell himself that he had to, and then he would remember his dad, who'd called him a quitter. Maybe he could face that part, but what he couldn't face was going back to Brigham City and admitting he had washed out of paratrooper school, that he was part of some regular "straight leg" infantry battalion. Infantrymen were the grunts of the military. To the guys back home, Airborne guys, or Marines, got respect, but a dogface in the infantry was nothing. Spence had bragged way too much. He had told everyone that he had passed his Airborne test, and he had spouted off about the paratroopers being the toughest soldiers. And then he had had to wait all winter, after he had thought he would be leaving, before the army could get him into basic training and jump school. All that time he had worked at odd jobs when he could, or just worked around the farm, but he had told the guys, "I could go in right now, if I wanted infantry, but I'm waiting for Airborne training." And he'd always gotten a reaction. He could see it in people's eyes, even when they didn't say much. Maybe he was small, but he was going into the paratroopers, and that made him feel a whole lot taller.

The last time he had seen LuAnn, he had told her, "Well, sure, the Airborne boys get themselves into some tight spots, but maybe that's what it's going to take to win this war. I can handle it all right." What was he supposed to do now, go back home and tell her that he hadn't been able to cut the mustard?

"It doesn't make any sense," Ted said, his voice barely a whisper. "If we do live through this, we'll get killed once we get into action."

"Maybe. Maybe not. From what I've heard, the best way to get home is to fight with a crack outfit. Those are the guys who know how to look out for each other."

"That's what the guy at the recruiting office told you, isn't it?"

"Well . . . yeah."

"That's what they told me, too. But you heard what Captain Vance said."

Spence had heard it, all right—had never stopped thinking about it. The recruits had piled off an old army bus and filed into this oven of a barracks, and then had baked there for almost an hour. When Vance had walked in, he wasn't even sweating. He was tall and hard, and his khakis were creased, sharp as scythe blades. He had stood there in front of the men, and in an even, sort of friendly voice, told them, "You've made a huge mistake coming here. If you have any sense at all, you'll drop out now."

It had seemed a kind of joke, and some of the men had smiled, but it didn't take long to know he meant it. "We're the shock troops of the army. We drop out of airplanes behind enemy lines. We fight surrounded. Chances are, if you stay with this unit, you'll die. If you have any sense at all, you'll quit right now. So who wants out?"

Captain Vance had waited, as though he expected some hands to go up, but no one had responded.

"The fact is, the war—even death—might not seem so bad after what we're going to put you through for the next thirteen weeks. You'll arise at four every morning, and you will fall into bed exhausted when the day is over. No weekend passes, no break, nothing but the hardest work you have ever done in your lives."

Captain Vance had waited then, stood straight, with Sergeant Moreno by his side, and he had let some of that sink in. "But don't worry," he had finally added. "You have a way out. You can drop out now, or anytime in the next three days. All you have to do is show a little good sense, tell us that you want to leave, and we'll send you away—no dishonor, no shame, no blot on your record."

He looked around at the men and nodded, as if to say, "See how reasonable I am." But then his voice got nasty—like that was the kind of guy he really was, all along—and he said, "But if you stay three days, and any day after that, decide to quit, you'll get what you deserve. We'll put you in our dog unit, and you'll work in the kitchen. You'll clean latrines and sweep floors, and if we catch you looking at the *real men*, straight in the eye, we'll remind you that you're a dog and that you have no such right. So quit now, gentlemen. I beg you to quit now, or quit tomorrow or the next day, but if you stay beyond that, just remember that I warned you."

Then Vance had stepped toward Spence, had stood almost on top of him. "Soldier, how old are you?" he had asked.

"Seventeen."

"What did you say to me?"

"Sir! I'm seventeen, sir."

"When are you going to start shaving?"

Someone laughed.

"Sir. I do shave, sir." Spence had stood stiff, barked the answer into the captain's face. That much he had learned already.

But the captain was looking at Ted by then. "What about you? How old are you?"

"Sir. Almost eighteen, sir." But that was not quite true. Ted was only about a month older than Spence.

"I want both of you to leave right now. Just tell me that you quit. We don't want little boys in this outfit."

Spence didn't say anything, and neither did Ted, although Vance continued to stare at them. Finally, he nodded, and stepped away. But then came the selling point: "I will say this, men. If you stick it out, you'll be the toughest, most hard-nosed troops in the world, and everyone will know it. You'll also be part of something new: this regiment is going to stay together—train and then fight together—and cut a swath through Europe, right to Hitler's throat. A lot of you won't come back, but those who do will know that they were part of the greatest fighting group ever created."

He had walked out then, and it was the sergeant who asked again which of the men wanted to quit.

Two men did. One was an older guy, a college man, who muttered, "This is for Neanderthals. I can go join up with the Nazis if I want to be treated like that."

But Spence had liked something about all the tough talk. This was his chance to prove to himself that he could handle something really hard.

Now, however—three days later—none of that seemed so important. All Spence could think was that he had thirteen weeks of torture ahead of him, and at the end, those towers were waiting. What he wished, more than anything, was that he had never come here, that he was still home in Brigham City, still in high school. He had never lived where the humidity was so high, had never been worked until he was sick enough to puke. On some of the double-time marches, men had collapsed. They hadn't quit on purpose; they had just fainted. Ambulances had followed the troops, the officers knowing the whole time that some would go down. "It's all right to pass out," Captain Vance had told them. "But if you quit, and step out of line, you'll be shipped off this base on the next bus. So run till you drop, but don't ever stop on purpose."

Spence's arms and shoulders ached from the push-ups, his legs throbbed, and a kind of tiredness he had never known was working its way into his head. But when Ted said, "Really. I can't do it, Spence. I'm at the end of my rope," Spence suddenly sat up and said, "Sure, you can. Let's get dressed and get something to eat. That'll help. Then we'll go to sleep as soon as we get back."

So they stuck it out, even though a bunch of guys quit that day. In another week the numbers of recruits had dropped by more than half, and the guys left in the regiment had crossed the Chattahoochee River to the Alabama side of the base. Conditions there were worse than they had been in the Frying Pan, and the training schedule was just as tough. "But we're getting stronger," Spence kept telling Ted. "We're doing things easy now that would've killed us those first couple of days."

One morning, Sergeant Moreno went a little easier on the men, called off the long run they normally made every other day. The recruits were happy. They ate extra helpings of spaghetti and meatballs at lunch. But then, as they walked from the mess hall, expecting only classroom time, and feeling almost human, Moreno had called them back together. "There's been a change. We run today, after all."

Spence saw Captain Vance standing in the distance, watching all this, and he knew this had been a setup all along, a rotten trick to break more of the men. The troops double-timed their full eight miles that day, in army boots and full packs, and they left a trail of vomit as all that spaghetti came back up. Spence had never known such pain in his life. He had thought two-a-day football practices had been tough in the August heat of Utah, but that seemed kid stuff now. He ran until he reached his breaking point, but he only bent a little and turned his head when he vomited, afraid that if he came to a stop, he would be forced from the ranks and sent from the unit. He was too mad to let that happen. He was not going to let Vance defeat him. At one point he grabbed hold of Ted and held him up, but he kept him going, too, and both of them finally made it back to the camp.

Eight more men quit that day, but Spence and Ted survived, and Spence knew that nothing would be harder. Long runs, after that one, seemed manageable, if not easy. And at some point Spence began to take pride in the way his body was hardening. He could knock off twenty-five push-ups with ease. He was also being filled with information and specialized training: care of weapons, sharpshooting, map reading, rules of engagement.

The trouble was, the jumps were still coming, and Spence's fear was building up. He didn't want to get through all this work and then turn chicken on the tower or up in an airplane. Back home, Spence had pictured a parachute drop as a gentle flight, like cotton drifting from a cotton-wood tree. But paratroopers dropped from low altitudes, and stories of hard drops, in wind, kept going around—guys breaking legs or ribs. Or stories of turbulence, of men puking up their guts in the back of a C-47.

But Spence made it through the first jump—from a forty-foot tower—and then he lived through a frightening slide down a wire, from 250 feet, and finally a real drop from that height. By the time he entered a C-47 for his first in-flight drop, he had himself convinced that a parachute jump wouldn't be so bad after all. Ted had struggled with the heights more than Spence had, and Spence found himself expending his concentration more on getting Ted through the first jump than worrying about himself. The men packed their own parachutes, and then they marched to the hangars in their heavy boots, their double chutes, front and back, but not with as much heavy equipment as they would someday actually carry in a combat jump.

It was enough. It was summer now, and they waited

in the heat of the hangar, sweating like draft horses, before they were finally marched to the airplane. Sixteen men made up one "stick" of jumpers, and Ted was fourth, Spence fifth, in the line. They boarded the airplane, fastened their seatbelts, and waited. Spence looked around at his friends, these men who had passed through this nightmare and were now on the brink of finishing their training. They were white, silent, nervous. No one said much.

Vic Barela, one of the older men in Spence's squad, a guy about twenty-five, did look across at Spence and Ted and say, "How come you two little fellows are taking such deep breaths. You're not scared, are you?"

Barela, along with a buddy of his named Whitesides, had been razzing Spence and Ted every day since the beginning. Spence hardly noticed anymore. "I just like this good smell in here," Spence said. "I was sniffing at it."

The smell was actually disgusting—all the sweating men, and the stink of the airplane fuel.

Barela grinned, but he was looking as pasty as anyone, as tense.

The airplane taxied into position, revved its engines, lumbered down the runway like a tired old goose, and then lifted slowly into the air. Spence felt it all in his stomach, and when the airplane hit the first pockets of turbulence, he was already close to losing his breakfast. But only a few minutes passed before the jumpmaster called, "Unfasten your seatbelts," and that took Spence's attention away from his stomach.

"Get ready!"

The men knew the commands; understood what they had to do. They had practiced this many times. And it was lucky they had. Spence felt as though his mind had quit working, that his body was simply running on automatic. He grabbed his snap fastener and held it in his right hand.

"Stand up!"

Spence got up and grabbed the cable over his head with his left hand. He turned toward the back of the airplane.

"Hook up!"

All the men reached up and snapped their fasteners over the cable. This would be the line that would release their parachutes as they jumped. They wouldn't have to pull the cord themselves.

"Check equipment!"

Each man made the ritual check of the trooper's chute in front of him, and then the shout came up the line: "Sixteen okay. Fifteen okay. Fourteen okay," and on through to the first man.

"Stand in the door!"

The trainees shuffled forward to the open hatch. The first man in the stick took his position, his hands gripped on either side of the door. In the pause that followed, fear finally hit Spence full force, and once again, he thought he was about to vomit. His heart was thumping in his ears, louder than the terrific noise of the airplane, all that wind in the open door. The thought struck him that when the first man went out, and the men moved forward, nothing would happen, that he was frozen in place. He was beginning to think what he would say, how he could explain away his cowardice when he had to drop out of line.

"Go!"

And just like that, the first man was out in the air and gone. Spence felt the resistance in Ted, his muscles seemingly locked up. It was pushing Ted forward that took Spence a step up. And then another jumper was out. And another. When Ted reached the door, Spence set his foot sideways behind Ted's left foot, for a brace. It was what they had practiced. The jumpmaster called "go" again and tapped Ted's leg, but he didn't move. That's when Spence pushed. Ted half jumped, half fell from the airplane, and then Spence stepped to the door. He felt the tap, but he made no decision; his body just did what it had been taught to do. He leaped and swung his left leg forward, made the quarter turn left he had practiced. Then the prop blast hit him, driving him down. He held his head forward, counted, "One one-thousand, two one-thousand . . ." Just then a force hit his shoulders with a powerful pull as the parachute opened. He was jarred almost to a stop, it seemed, and the parachute risers caught his steel helmet, jerking it hard against the back of his neck. But he looked up and saw the white canopy over his head, and he was relieved.

He hardly had time to think, to enjoy the ride. He took hold of the front risers, looked toward the horizon, and held his feet together, his legs slightly bent. At the last second he pulled the risers to slow his descent, but he had lost all sense of where he was, and suddenly the ground was there and his parachute was pulling him forward. He leaned back, hard, and slammed onto his backside, felt the air go out of him. It was not a good landing, not by the book at all, but he was on the ground. And he remembered what to do: collapse the canopy, roll up the chute, and then hustle off the drop zone.

He felt relieved, even sort of excited—until he saw Ted. Ted had gotten down first, but he was a little slower making it to the formation. He ran toward Spence, stopping in front of him. "I can't do that again," he said. "I *won't* do it again."

Spence hadn't really thought about that yet. He couldn't think how he could go back up the next morning and go through all that again. In fact, four more times— and the last one in the dark.

CHAPTER 5

It was September 1944. Dieter Hedrick was fifteen.
For a month now he had been living in Luxembourg, near
the Mosel River, just across the border from Germany. He
was working with crews of Hitler Youth, digging antitank
trenches along the *Westwall*—sometimes called the Siegfied
Line. Since D-Day, in June, the Americans, British, and
Canadians had been pushing out of Normandy and now
were rolling across France. Dieter was doing his part to
make certain that foreign troops never crossed into his
country. Some parts of the *Westwall* had been cannibal-
ized earlier to create fortifications on the French coast,
but those lines had now been breached. The final wall of
protection had to be fortified. German forces were prepar-
ing to make their heroic stand.

Dieter had known for a long time that the enemy must
never enter Germany. He knew how vicious American

and British soldiers would be. Their pilots had been bombing German cities—killing civilians—for years. So what would stop them from raping and killing women, gunning down children or old people? Every German had been warned about this. What Dieter wished was that he could put down his shovel and take up a rifle. He hoped, more than anything, that he could soon be part of the regular army, or better yet, be placed in a military SS unit. It was one thing to dig a ditch, but it was greater to face the enemy—to kill his share of the stinking Americans—*Amis*, as Germans called them—who would soon be coming in hoards.

Dieter had grown tall in the last five years. He was a strong boy, too, and known for his commitment to the *HJ—Hitler Jugend* and to the *Führer*. He was already a *Scharführer*—a troop leader—and the one his commander, Rolf Braun, relied on most often. Dieter was not a great athlete, but he had competed ferociously for his *HJ* teams. He had also distinguished himself at his three-week weapons training camp during the previous spring, and then had spent much of the summer in Augsburg as part of an antiaircraft battery. All through Germany now, Hitler Youth as young as thirteen were operating searchlights, even firing AA guns. Dieter's crew had had one definite kill to its credit, and, he suspected, several more. His crew had worked tirelessly after raids, too, cleaning up debris in the city and helping bombed-out families find shelter. What he understood was that the superiority of the German people was being tested to the limit, but he also knew that it would, in the end, prevail. The Allies didn't have the will to push all the way into Germany. They would be driven back, finally, just as the stinking Russians would be in the east, and then his determination would all be worth it. He could already see the day coming when he would be a great leader in the Third Reich.

When Dieter's Hitler Youth section had arrived in Traben, on the Mosel River, his commander had immediately shut down a local school and converted it to sleeping quarters for about half the boys. Rolf Braun was only seventeen, but he was the leader of 180 young men, and he was fearless. When the principal of the school had refused to leave, Braun had told Dieter, in a firm, controlled voice, "Get some help if you need it. Then throw this man out of here. If he gives you trouble, or if he tries to return, shoot him."

Dieter was not surprised by the order. He found another boy, and the two took hold of the elderly principal, one on each arm, and delivered him into the street. When the man swore at the boys, Dieter pulled his Walther pistol from his holster and pointed it at him. "Don't think I won't shoot," he said as coldly as he could. "Get going."

And the man walked away.

It was an amazing feeling, this power, and the whole town soon knew it. Rank-and-file Hitler Youth weren't supposed to abuse the local citizens. Only the leaders had authority to take command, but the boys were spread out across a long distance, and Dieter heard reports of fourteen-year-old boys demanding what they wanted from the locals. Most of the boys didn't have weapons, but they had numbers, and they had reputation. They could usually get what they wanted.

Dieter certainly would have shot the old man had it become necessary. But that was not wrong. Discipline had to be kept, and *HJ* leaders had to show, from the beginning, that they were not children, that they represented the *Reich*, and as such, were in charge of the village. But there was no reason to be ruthless. A noble leader did what he had to do, but he never forgot the greatness of Germany, the responsibility of a proud, young Aryan and follower of Hitler.

It didn't take long, after arrival, for Dieter to find out what kind of leader he was. One afternoon he was walking along a trench, inspecting the work, when he heard someone shouting. He was startled at first, but as he ran toward the sound, he was even more surprised to hear laughter. He was practically on top of one of his crews before the boys spotted him. As they did, they spun around and came to attention.

"What's this? What's going on here?"

"Nothing, *Herr Scharführer*," one of the boys gasped. "We were only . . ." But he didn't dare finish.

What the boys had been up to was unthinkable. Mud was spattered over their uniforms. Clearly, they had been playing around, probably tossing globs of mud at each other.

"Out! Out of the trench!" Dieter screamed.

The boys were some of the youngest ones in his group. Of the four, three were still fourteen. The other was about Dieter's age. They scrambled out of the trench, and then they stood at attention again.

"Is this what you do to honor the *Führer*?" Dieter demanded. "Do you waste your time—and dishonor your uniforms?"

The oldest boy, Ernst Gessell, said, "We've been working hard all day, Dieter. We didn't intend any—"

"What did you call me?"

"I'm sorry. *Herr Scharführer*."

"Has it come to this? Are you nothing but little boys, playing in the mud?"

"No, *Herr Scharführer*. Look how much we've done today. We've made good progress."

"How much more *could* you have done?"

The boys knew better than to respond. They all stood silent, still breathing hard, waiting. Dieter had to make a decision. If he reported them, they would be punished. It was even possible—if Braun was in a bad mood—that they might be sent to the eastern front as infantry soldiers. But Dieter was also well aware that such a report was a bad reflection on himself, and he didn't want that. "You will work two hours extra tonight. You will miss your dinner. And you will thank me every day, as long as we stay here, that I didn't turn you in. You know what that could mean."

"Yes, yes. We do thank you," Gessell said. "We'll work very hard for you. We'll make you look good."

"Gessell! Think what you're saying! We have very little time left to get this job done. Do you understand how important this is?"

"*Ja, Herr Scharführer,*" they all said in unison.

"We're friends. Good friends. But you have to know, if this happens again, I'll report you instantly. And I can't answer for what will happen to you."

Again, they responded in unison, and Dieter liked what he felt. These were not bad boys. He had appealed to their sense of honor, and they had understood. He had frightened them, too, of course, and that would make them think twice before they were tempted to act this way again. Over all, he was very pleased with the way he had managed the situation.

Two weeks later, a British Spitfire suddenly dove through the clouds and made a long run over the trench. The boys scattered for the trees nearby, but the fighter strafed with machine guns, and a number of boys went down. But only one was killed. Ernst Gessell.

The adult commander of the entire operation—

Oberleutnant Feiertag—gave a wonderful speech at Gessell's burial. He told the boys they could consider themselves soldiers now. One of their ranks had fallen, and now everyone was part of the heroic battle to save their country. Hitler had never wanted war, but he had stood up for the rights of Germans—not only those in the Fatherland, but those ethnic Germans who lived in other lands. England had always hated Germany, had held them down since the First World War, and now was trying to destroy them again with their bombing raids. Roosevelt had brought America into the war only because he was hungry for power himself. He wanted to hold Germany down so that America could dominate the world. "What you will find," Feiertag told the boys, "is that in every land where our people have been abused and mistreated, Jews have been behind the trouble. The Jews seek to control the world's money, to mongrelize our population by marrying with pure Aryan people. The day will come when the pure race will finally hold its rightful position in the world. We have no desire to dominate anyone, but only to lead, as we are *destined* to do. And Ernst Gessell, this noble young man, has done his small part to bring about that destiny. We may all give our lives before the battle is won, but if we do, we can go to our rest knowing that our purpose was great, our motivation pure."

Dieter didn't cry. He wouldn't allow himself that. But he was moved. And he was satisfied. Had he turned

Gessell in, after the unfortunate incident, the boy would have been dishonored and disgraced. Instead, he had died valiantly for his country.

But Dieter had seen his friend Ernst after the machine gun had torn him up. A slab of flesh had ripped from his side. His ribs had been twisted and pulled halfway from his body, and his intestines had hung out in a bloody clump. There had been a stench coming from his body, something tart and rotten. Dieter couldn't help wondering what Ernst had felt, how much pain he had experienced, before he died. Dieter certainly was willing to die, but his idea of an honorable death had always been glorious and clean. Ernst Gessell's flesh had been real: like mangled meat lying on a roadside. Dieter couldn't get that picture out of his head.

That night, in his room alone, Dieter let his mind drift back to his home in Bavaria. He thought of the willow trees along the river, the leaves turning yellow now, the sheep along the green hillsides. The night before Dieter had left home, his mother had sat with him in the kitchen, at the table. He had told her not to regret that he was leaving, that young men had to grow up early in time of war. She had cried, and she had told him, "Dieter, you know nothing. You only know what these Hitler Youth leaders tell you. A boy should play football. He should go to school, have a girlfriend, go walking with his family on Sunday afternoons. These Nazis are going to get you killed."

It was shocking talk, and Dieter had been ashamed. "You can't say that to me, Mother. You know how wrong it is," he had told her, and he knew that according to regulation, he should have reported her. But he had felt sorry for her. She wasn't a smart woman, not very well educated, had only known life in a little village and on the farm. So she could be forgiven. But now, as he sat in his room, he thought about the way she had clung to him that night and sobbed, the way she had gripped him around the back with her soft arms.

Dieter thought, too, of his family at the train station on the morning he had departed from Krumbach. His father had said nothing, not a word. He had offered a handshake, a nod of the head, but the rest was all in his eyes. Dieter's sisters and his little brother had cried, and Mother had held him again, but Father had looked resolute. Someone watching might have thought he was proud and satisfied, but Dieter knew better. Father had no vision. He was angry. He liked his farm, liked to be on his own; he had no sense of history, not enough concern for what Germany could become.

Still, Dieter missed his family, missed even the early breakfasts, before school, and the smell of cows from the barn, just a step outside the kitchen. He missed fresh eggs and milk, bacon, even missed his giggling little sisters. It was so weak of him to worry about such things in this great time, when every ounce of concentration had to be brought to the purpose at hand. But it was better than thinking of Gessell, with his guts flopping in the dirt.

All autumn the boys continued to dig. As some of the older boys were sent to bolster troops on the nearby front, younger boys took over the leadership. Dieter was called to serve in place of Braun, as the leader of the entire section of 180 boys: *Gefolgshaftsführer*. He was the youngest of the leaders to reach such a rank, at least here in this part of the *Westwall*, and he was proud of the honor.

But more boys meant more trouble, and troubles were definitely mounting. The crews had been told that they were called to serve for only sixty days, but that time had passed and still the boys were digging—and from all appearance, would be for some time yet. Lieutenant Feiertag warned the Hitler Youth leaders that they had to be vigilant. "We've started to have a few run off," he said. "We must put a stop to it or we'll lose control here. Watch your boys closely, and if you see signs of trouble, clamp down before it's too late."

"What will happen to boys who run?" one of the leaders asked.

Feiertag shook his head sadly. "We have no choice. Anyone we catch, we'll have to shoot. We have to show the others that we have only one way we deal with treason, no matter what the age of the traitor."

Dieter took that message to his boys, shouted it into

their faces, and he didn't worry much that any of his boys would try to run. He found a boy weeping one day, saying that he wanted to go home, but Dieter had a long talk with him, bolstered his self-confidence, and felt good when the young man went back to work.

And then one morning, early, one of Dieter's *Scharführer* knocked at his door. Dieter got up and let the boy in. "Yes, what is it?" he demanded. He got little enough sleep as it was, without someone waking him long before daylight.

"We have someone missing," the boy said. His face was white with panic. "Willi Hofmann is gone. We've looked everywhere for him. He took all his things and he cleared out."

"Can we track him? He must be on foot."

"I don't know. His friend said he had some money. Maybe he took a train."

Dieter spent most of the day searching, but he couldn't pick up his old friend's trail, and so he was forced to make a report. Dieter was ashamed, of course. One of his boys had taken off, and that didn't speak well for his leadership. "This must not happen again," Lieutenant Feiertag told him. "Call your boys together and let them know what Hofmann's going to get. He's almost sure to go home, and when he does, we'll bring him back here to shoot him."

Dieter wondered whether that would happen. Willi

had never been serious about much of anything, and he certainly wasn't Dieter's idea of a traitor. He was not very smart, either, but would he be stupid enough to go home?

For a week Dieter watched his boys, warned them every time he got a chance, and he worried about Willi. He knew it would be better for the project if the boy was caught. That would be something Dieter could tell his crews, use as a warning. But he found himself hoping that Willi could disappear somewhere. Dieter had known him all his life. They had gone to the same school, had gone through *Jungvolk* and *HJ* together, had hiked together, gone into the cold water together when most of the boys were scared. And another memory kept haunting Dieter. Once, during a camping trip, Dieter had eaten his food and was still hungry. Willi had carried more food along than Dieter, and had offered him some bread and a piece of cheese. It was nothing special, but Willi was a friend, and now he had shamed himself, turned his back on his country.

Another few days went by, and then Lieutenant Feiertag showed up at Dieter's headquarters. "We have Hofmann," he said. "He's on his way here."

"Did he go home?"

"No. He went to his uncle's house, and his crazy uncle put him up, tried to hide him. Now the man's going to serve two years in prison for harboring a deserter."

"What about Hofmann?" Dieter asked.

"We'll shoot him, of course. Get your troops together."

"Why?"

"So they can watch."

"Watch?"

"Yes. Of course. What's the point of making an example of him if the boys don't see it themselves? No one else will be running off from your section, I can tell you that."

Dieter gave the Nazi salute and said, "*Heil*, Hitler." He got on his motorcycle and made the trip down his lines. He let all his leaders know that they must assemble their troops that evening, at a point near Dirnsdorf. He didn't tell them why. He didn't want too much talk. All the boys in Dieter's unit from back home knew Willi, had known him all their lives.

That afternoon Dieter arrived at the farmhouse that Feiertag used for his headquarters, and he walked inside. There was Willi sitting in the little living room, his hands and feet manacled. His eyes were fixed. He seemed not to see Dieter—or anything else. And Dieter couldn't stand to look at him. He walked back out. By then, other boys were arriving. These sorts of gatherings were not common, and everyone seemed curious. Dieter heard some speculating about what was going on, and before long the truth spread through the crowd. Dieter watched as boys got the news and then grew silent. He heard one boy say, "Why do we have to watch?" But no one answered.

Finally Feiertag assembled the boys. Then he stood before them. "What is about to happen," he said, "is very sad. I take no joy in this—none at all. Nor should anyone. Hitler Youth is made up of young patriots. When one of us shames himself, we are all shamed at least a little. If this were not a time of war, we could drive a coward from us and merely feel sorry for him that he has no more self-respect. But in time of war, when a man runs from battle, he represents a danger to every one of us. And so we have no choice about what we do here today. I wanted you to be here—all of you—to see this, not because we are happy to take this young man's life but because it shows our resolve, proves it, establishes that we will do whatever it takes to preserve our land."

Feiertag gestured, and four men, all soldiers—not Hitler Youth—walked outside. Two led the way, and two more had hold of Willi Hofmann. He was still not seeing anything, it seemed, still walking like a sleepwalker. But when the men began to tie him to a post, he came alive. He began to flail about, to fight against the bindings. The four men had to hang on to him, even slam him about a little, to get him tied up.

Dieter held his position, and he watched his boys. He finally turned to them and said, "No one break rank. No one fall out. Stand where you are."

But he saw their fear. And he felt the sickness that was rolling in his own stomach.

Hofmann continued to struggle, grunting and twisting, trying to break loose. The soldiers lined up and prepared to shoot, but the boy managed, in his terror, to pull the bindings loose. He couldn't get away, but he was tossing back and forth wildly, crying and screaming. "I'm sorry. I'm sorry. I'll stay this time. I'll work. I'll never run again."

And then a machine pistol began to pop, and blood spattered wildly. Hofmann's chest ripped open, and his throat. His clothes tore apart. He let out a shriek and then slumped forward against the ropes. Feiertag had not waited for the firing squad, not with all this wild flailing. He had simply ended everything with his own trigger finger.

But the gurgling continued, the sucking sound in Willi's chest.

Dieter gulped, tried to get his breath. He knew he had to accept this.

Dieter heard someone retch, heard a splat hit the ground, and that only set off others. In another moment, ten, then twenty or more, were down on their knees, vomiting on the ground.

And Lieutenant Feiertag was saying, "That's all right, boys. Don't be ashamed that you have to vomit. No one wanted this to happen. No one likes to see it." He paused for a time as the gurgling continued, the vomiting, and then he added, "May I trust now that not one of you will think of turning from his duty?"

CHAPTER 6

The weather had turned cold, had been all through November, and now the month was nearly over. But still, the trenches were not completed. Dieter saw little enthusiasm in his boys now. They were tired of the daily drudgery, the long hours and the bad weather. But no one complained—not since they had seen what had happened to Willi. Discipline had tightened all along the *Westwall*, and rumors circulated about boys who had slacked off, been caught dawdling, and had been immediately shipped to the eastern front to fight the Russians—with winter coming on. Some said there was little difference between that and a death penalty. The Russians were rampaging across eastern Europe now, pushing the German army back. Germany's newspapers claimed that the tide was about to turn, that soldiers would never let the Russians cross onto homeland soil, and Dieter believed that, but he was shocked by the retreat of German troops both in the east and west.

The older *HJ* boys were now being pulled out of the trenches and sent to fight as replacements on the nearby western front. The boys who were sixteen expected to join *Wehrmacht* or military SS troops once the ditches were finished. And that was Dieter's hope, even though he was still fifteen. He didn't want to be sent home, like a little boy; he wanted to be part of the action at the border, and then to see the turn of events as his countrymen took back control of the war. German troops were now gathering behind the *Westwall* with tanks and artillery. The soldiers were camped in the towns and fields in the section Dieter managed, and he heard from his leaders that German forces were also gathering all along the Luxembourg and Belgian borders. They weren't digging in, either. "They aren't taking defensive positions," Lieutenant Feiertag told Dieter. "Officers tell me, on the quiet, that they believe our troops are getting ready to attack."

It was a heady idea. For many months now, German troops had been pushed back, but now that was over. And Dieter, after talking to Feiertag, thought he saw what was coming. At the beginning of the war, Germans had cut through the Ardennes Forest in Belgium—where no one had expected them—and then turned south, defeated France in only a few weeks, and driven English troops back across the Channel. Hitler had drawn out the Americans and British, stretching them across western Europe. Now, it appeared, he would go after them, once again through the Ardennes. It made such perfect sense. Meanwhile, the ignorant Russians, also stretched too far from their homeland, and giving up millions of lives as they fought, would finally spend their power, and Germans, with ten times the will of the Russians, would drive them back too. Dieter had heard it all from his Hitler Youth leaders before he had left home: What looked like a disaster for Germany was about to turn. It couldn't be otherwise. Germany couldn't—*wouldn't*—be defeated.

Late one evening Dieter received a telephone call at his headquarters. He got out of bed to answer the phone, and he was still only half awake when the caller identified himself as a military officer, not a Hitler Youth leader. Suddenly Dieter was alert. But the officer's message was nothing surprising. "You are called to a conference in the morning. Early. You'll be picked up at five. Be outside."

"Yes, sir," Dieter said, and he was about to hang up the phone.

But then the man said, "Be certain you shine your boots. Wear your best uniform."

"Of course." It was what Dieter would have done anyway. What Hitler Youth leader would ever attend a meeting without looking his best?

He did arise very early the next morning, however,

and he cleaned and shined his boots a little more carefully than he might have otherwise, and he took out his best uniform, the one he wore only to such gatherings, and he brushed it, made certain it looked tidy.

At five o'clock he was outside when a dark Mercedes pulled up in front of his quarters. He got inside and greeted a young officer from the *Waffen SS*. The man seemed to know very little, and didn't have much to say, so Dieter rode in silence, alone in the back. He wasn't really sure where the car traveled in the dark, but he knew it was heading into the Hunsrück range of mountains. This was unusual. Dieter had never been pulled so far from his work, never returned so far east into Germany. He could only assume that the meeting must involve many more leaders than those in the sector where he was working.

Eventually, after passing through a couple of guard stations, where the driver had to stop and show passes and personal papers, the car headed along a gravel road that cut through a densely wooded area. A wet snow had been falling off and on, not amounting to much, but the day was grim. What Dieter saw eventually was not a building but an armored train that was parked on a side track. There were only a few cars, and yet they were con- nected to a large, modern diesel engine, and the train was equipped with an 88-millimeter antiaircraft gun.

When Dieter stepped from the Mercedes, an SS major checked his papers and relieved him of his pistol. Dieter, for the first time, was frightened. Had he been accused of something? Was he being arrested? He walked past a row of SS soldiers, all with automatic weapons, some with guard dogs, and then entered one of the cars of the train. There he found three other Hitler Youth leaders and some of the SS overseers who were directing the massive *Westwall* project, but the inside of the train was even more surprising than the outside. It was paneled in oak, fitted with chandeliers, and with a beautiful mosaic of inlaid wood across the ceiling.

Dieter looked around at the other boys, who seemed as mystified as he was. No one spoke. Over the next few minutes two more Hitler Youth leaders arrived, both well dressed and equally impressed as they entered the car and stepped onto the plush, blue carpet. By then other SS and army officials had entered the car: two generals and several colonels. Only something marvelous could happen here, but still, Dieter couldn't think what it was. And then the door opened, and a man stepped in. Dieter recognized Albert Speer, one of the highest officials in the government of the Third Reich. He was the Minister of Armaments, in charge of the vast project of keeping German troops armed and ready for battle. Even the trench-digging project at the *Westwall* was ultimately under his command.

Speer smiled at the boys, nodded. They all leaped to attention, thrust their arms forward in the Nazi salute, and shouted, "*Heil*, Hitler!"

He returned the salute, casually, and he smiled. He was a delicate man with dark, tranquil eyes and heavy eyebrows. He stood before the boys and thanked them for their excellent work in their sector, for meeting their goals in spite of the bad weather they had suffered. Dieter felt lifted, as though his feet were off the floor. His work had been worth it, and this was his reward, to be thanked in person by such a highly placed leader.

Speer spoke to the boys a few minutes. He told them that the German army was about to take its stand, that a great moment in history was at hand. "We must stop the enemy. We will do it at the *Westwall*. Your work will never be forgotten by the German people." What he added, then, was that the work was not quite finished, and he was asking these leaders to pick up the pace—to extend working hours, and to complete the final stages of the project by December 10. The boys promised they would do it, and Dieter committed in his own heart that if he didn't sleep another minute between now and then, his crews would finish their part of the project.

All this was enough, but then Speer motioned to the door. "Young men," he said, "there is someone here who wants to meet you and thank you for your work. He has a medal he wishes to present to you."

The door opened at the end of the car, and Dieter held his breath. But he wasn't ready for what he saw. His knees almost went out from under him. The man stepping through the door was Adolf Hitler. With more awe than volume, the boys raised their arms and gasped, *"Heil, mein Führer."*

The *Führer* raised his arm quickly, from the elbow, and returned the salute. He walked over and faced the boys, who were standing in a line. Dieter had seen Hitler once before, from a distance, but never this way, standing within arm's length. But the *Führer* looked tired, and Dieter's heart went out to him. The man had been through so much. Only a few months before, a group of treacherous German generals had tried to assassinate him and had narrowly missed their mark. Hitler had the weight of this war on his shoulders, more than anyone, and Dieter was only thankful that he was one follower who was doing his share, not someone who had to face this, the greatest man in the world, in shame.

Hitler congratulated the boys in that strong voice Dieter had heard so many times on the radio. He told them they were heroes, that they had done a wonderful job. And then his voice took on a hint of the power he could unleash at his great mass meetings. "We are about to begin a major offensive, and I promise you, we will not be denied. We'll not only defend ourselves; we'll drive our enemies back from our borders."

Dieter was right. This was what he had been telling himself. But now the *Führer* had said it, so it would be so.

Hitler then walked down the line, stopped in front

of each boy. When he came to Dieter, he took his hand. Dieter was surprised at the filmy look in the *Führer*'s eyes, at the uneven shave, the patch of missed whiskers on his chin, but he concentrated on the words: "Son, I know I can count on you. Bavarian boys are made of strong stuff."

"Jawohl, mein Führer," Dieter said, but only in a whisper. He knew that this was the finest moment of his life, and always would be. He tried to draw it all in, think of the words, remember them. Then the *Führer* handed Dieter the medal. It was a War Service Cross, First Class, with Swords. If Dieter and the others had been members of the military, they might have received an Iron Cross, but this was the highest honor they could receive as civilians.

It was all Dieter could do not to make a fool of himself and shed tears, but he stood firm and strong. Then the boys, still in a line, marched from the train car. And outside, Dieter could see that everyone felt just as he did. The boys all stopped and looked back at the train, as though they wanted to memorize everything they had seen and experienced. But no one said a word.

For the next two weeks Dieter pushed his crews beyond sixty hours, beyond all reason, really. He had learned to be harsh when he had to be, and his boys knew better than to defy him. But they finished their part of the assignment, on schedule, and that meant they could be home for Christmas. Dieter was glad that the others would be leaving the front before the Allies attacked, but that's not what he wanted for himself. He needed, somehow, to get in on the battle.

Every day he talked with Lieutenant Feiertag and told him that even though he was not yet sixteen, he had proved himself in his command. Now he deserved the chance to prove himself on the field of battle. His words always seemed to fall on deaf ears, but then, on the last day before the boys were to board their train back home, Feiertag came to him, smiling. "All right. You got what you wanted. You're going to the front."

Dieter took a long breath. He was excited, and . . . something else. He didn't want to admit that he was frightened—didn't admit it—but that night he found he was too excited to sleep and, as he pictured the combat, he did worry a little. Would he actually bring honor to himself when the time came? This was no longer about fancy words and stated commitments. Now he had to put his life on the line, for real. He couldn't let himself down, couldn't fail the *Führer*.

Early the next morning Dieter wrote to his family, telling them of the honor he had received: the medal, and the chance to join the fight. He knew what his parents would think, how reticent they would be about this, and it angered him a little. But when he mentioned Christmas, and told his parents that he wouldn't be home, he felt a certain sense of loss. He thought of his little brother, Gerhardt, who was twelve now, almost thirteen. Gerhardt would be disappointed that Dieter wasn't coming home. Dieter wondered when he would see the boy again, and have a chance to tell him all the things he had seen and done. He even found himself hoping—and feeling guilty as he did so—that Gerhardt could stay home for a few years yet, not be drawn into the war. There was nothing wrong, of course, with hoping the war would end soon and that no more German boys would have to die, but Dieter knew he was actually thinking more of Christmas and of the days when he hadn't had so much to worry about. He wanted Gerhardt to have some more years of that kind.

That morning Dieter also said good-bye to the boys under his command. He noticed no show of love from them, and he understood why—even though it bothered him a little. Couldn't they understand that he had had no choice but to drive them hard? He was taken by truck that afternoon and dropped off at a camp near Aachen. He and some other boys who had not returned home were given gear and uniforms and a place to sleep, and then they spent the next day being processed into the army. On the following morning he and the others were hauled south to another camp and, without any training other than what they had received in Hitler Youth, were suddenly members of a company of soldiers in the Forty-seventh *Panzer* Corps, part of the Fifteenth Army.

A young *Feldwebel*—a sergeant—took Dieter to a tent, helped him stow his equipment, and then said, "This is Corporal Schaefer. He'll look after you—tell you what to do."

A big man, older—maybe forty-five or so—was sitting on his cot. He was dark-haired, except for some graying around his ears. His whiskers, not shaved for a few days, were also tinted with gray. But what Dieter saw was the lifelessness in his eyes, his face, the absence of interest in Dieter's arrival. He was sitting on a little stool, and he had a sheet of paper on his lap, with a wooden ammunition box under it, for a writing surface. He had apparently been writing a letter.

"I'm Dietrich Hedrick," Dieter said, and he held out his hand.

Schaefer looked toward Dieter but didn't seem to see him. "Johann Schaefer," he said. He gave Dieter's hand a quick shake.

"I'm glad to be here. From all I hear, something big could be coming in this sector."

Schaefer's eyes finally focused on Dieter. "How old are you?" he asked.

Dieter couldn't bring himself to tell the truth. His sixteenth birthday was not so many months off, however, so he said, "Sixteen, but I've been commanding one-hundred eighty men for months now. We've been fortifying the *Westwall*."

"Hitler Youth?"

"Yes." Dieter saw the doubt in the man's eyes, the skepticism. "Don't worry about me, Corporal," he said. "I'm ready to fight. I know I'm young, but I'm not afraid."

"That's just the trouble," Schaefer said softly, but not with any interest. He looked back to his paper.

"I don't mean that I'll be rash. I won't take chances. I'll follow you experienced men and learn from your example."

Schaefer was writing now, not seeming to notice that Dieter was talking.

"Is this a strong unit, the Forty-seventh?"

Schaefer was once again slow to react, but finally, without looking up, he said, "No. It isn't. It's patched together. We're only at about half strength. We're short on tanks and trucks and artillery. And we have no air support."

Dieter was stunned to hear a German soldier say such a thing. "Surely, such negative talk won't help matters, Corporal," Dieter said. "Surprise—and courage—can make up for other shortages."

Schaefer looked up once again, and this time he focused clearly on Dieter, studied him. "You shouldn't be here, a young boy like you," he said, his voice actually taking on a kindly tone.

"I'll fight as well as anyone in the company. I promise you that."

"You don't know that. You have no idea what you'll do. You don't understand what you've gotten yourself into here."

And now there was not just kindness but sadness in the man's voice. Dieter was unnerved. He turned away. He began unpacking his bag of equipment. Schaefer had the wrong attitude, of course; there could be no question about that. But the man didn't sound like a bad person. Maybe he was simply discouraged. Dieter decided not to judge him too severely. He finished arranging his things, and then he asked, "Where have you fought before, Corporal?"

"Russia."

"How did you end up on this front?"

Schaefer seemed hesitant to have this conversation, but he said, "I was shot through the chest. I was in a hospital for eight months. When I got out, they sent me here."

"You've been through plenty, Corporal. You're a hero—a great German hero. It's an honor for me to fight alongside you."

Schaefer may have smiled, just a hint, but he didn't say anything. Dieter knew what he must be thinking: that Dieter was all talk but not someone worthy to fight with grown men. He thought of telling Schaefer about the medal he had received from the *Führer* himself, of the danger he had already faced in the trenches. But this old corporal may only see that as more talk. Dieter knew the only proof would come when he showed his valor under fire. But he couldn't resist saying, "Corporal, you'll learn to trust me. I promise you that. I'm not afraid to die."

"It's not death that's frightening," Schaefer said. "You'll soon find out what's worse."

The words penetrated, and took some of Dieter's breath away. "I'll be all right," he said quietly, after a moment. But he felt a strange gloom come over him. He hadn't expected such a thing, not after meeting Adolf Hitler himself, not after vowing his allegiance to the *Führer*, face-to-face. Dieter knew he had to be careful. Soldiers like Schaefer were dangerous. They could break down a man's resolve. His leaders in *HJ* had warned him about such people.

CHAPTER 7

For the next few days Schaefer didn't say much, but when he did speak, he almost always had something negative to say. Dieter finally decided he had heard enough. The man had been through a lot, but he was a dangerous influence on the entire company. Dieter went to the company commander, Captain Schmidt. He quoted Corporal Schaefer word for word, described his sentiments about the operation that was about to begin, and then he said, "If we go into battle, how can we tolerate a man like that? His attitude could infect the others. It's the sort of pessimism that could destroy us."

The captain was sitting at his desk in a big field tent. He let Dieter stand before him, straight and correct, and for a time he merely stared at him. But then he said, "Hedrick, you let me worry about Schaefer."

"But it's your responsibility to—"

Schmidt suddenly stood up. "Don't ever try to tell me what my responsibility is, young man. You worry about your own."

"Yes, sir."

"And I'll tell you this. Schaefer knows more about fighting than you ever will. You stay close to him and listen to everything he tells you. Then I won't have to worry about you. If I could ship you out of here right now, I would. I don't need children in my company."

Dieter was stunned. Shamed. He couldn't believe a *Wehrmacht* officer could say such a thing—*think* such a thing.

"Now get out of here."

Dieter saluted and said, "*Heil*, Hitler" with force—as a rebuke. The day would come when he would prove himself as a soldier, and then he would see that heads rolled in this company. He hadn't met a soldier he was sure he could count on yet. Too many of them grumbled and complained. If any of these men had had to stand before the *Führer*, as Dieter had done, they would hang their heads. But he was finished with trying to change them. He would lead by example and hope for the best. It was becoming clearer every day that preparations were over and a battle was coming. Brave men would have to step forward then and show the others what was needed.

That afternoon Captain Schmidt called the company together. The soldiers stood outside in the cold as he spoke to them in a voice that seemed to Dieter entirely too soft, too calm. "Men, we start our campaign in the morning," he began. "We'll cross the river with our tanks ahead of us. But we must keep up with the tanks, and they will be moving fast. The idea is to surprise the *Amis* and make a powerful forward thrust. Our battalion will lead out and forge a salient that other battalions will fill."

Dieter liked the idea, and he was pleased when Schmidt's voice took on a little more force. "Men, this is very important. These Americans across the way are the weakest troops in Europe. They're spread thin, and they're inexperienced. If we come with full force, they'll back away. They'll turn and run. What we're part of is the great reversal of the war. This will be something you can tell your grandchildren—that you were the ones who stopped the losses, turned the war around."

So the captain was not such a coward after all. This was the sort of speech Dieter had been hoping for. What he didn't like was what he saw around him. The men were silent. No one cheered or shouted, "*Heil*, Hitler," as Dieter wanted to do. The soldiers stood in the cold, their breaths puffing steam into the air, and they hardly moved. Dieter wondered why he hadn't been sent to an SS unit so that he could be among men who truly loved the *Führer*.

Back at the tent, after the meeting, Schaefer helped Dieter, showed him what to take and what to leave behind. Dieter knew better than to say too much about the next day's battle, but he did say, "Corporal, that was a fine speech the captain gave, wasn't it?"

"I've heard lots of speeches," Schaefer said.

"But don't you think it's brilliant, this surprise? The last thing the Americans expect is for us to attack. They'll be caught off guard, for certain."

"Maybe. But listen to me. When we move out, you stay with me. Don't do anything foolish. Let the tanks do the work. If I drop to the ground, you drop. Don't start running into battle without looking where you're going."

"I'd rather be too brave than too cautious, Corporal. No one ever won a war by acting like a scared little rabbit."

Suddenly Schaefer's hand shot out and gripped the front of Dieter's coat. The big man jerked Dieter close, and he spoke into his face, his stinking breath coming in gusts. "You win wars by killing *them*. The *Amis*," he shouted into Dieter's face. "Not by getting *yourself* killed. And if you think those Americans are a bunch of scared rabbits, you don't know what you're talking about. They don't want to die either. They want to kill you."

"I know all that. I'm not about to get myself shot for no reason."

Schaefer let go, pushed him away. But then he said, his voice much quieter, "You're a boy. You shouldn't be here. You shouldn't be out there until you have enough sense to protect yourself. With your attitude, there's no way you'll be alive for more than a few days."

These last words sank in. Dieter sat down on his cot. He didn't want to pay any attention to Schaefer, but the picture of his mother came to mind again. He saw her, that last day before he had left home, crying and begging him to be careful. He did want to see her again, did want to see his farm.

"Have you ever had a woman?"

"What?"

"You heard me."

"It's none of your business what I've done. I've done plenty, that's for sure."

"You haven't. You don't know anything. You haven't seen anything. All you know is what you've been filled up with in Hitler Youth. You need to survive this, go home, have a wife, a nice long life." Schaefer sat down on his cot, across from Dieter, and looked at him. "Hedrick, if you don't drop when I tell you to drop, I'll knock you down. It doesn't matter whether I come back or not, but if I can do anything about it, you will. I see you boys—this whole generation—dying, dying for nothing, and it breaks my heart."

Behind Schaefer's anger was another tone: weariness, perhaps, but also affection. It confused Dieter. He didn't want to let someone like this make him forget everything he had learned. The man was wrong. He had lost sight of the purpose of this war. It didn't matter that he was a nice man, in his own way; he was still dangerous.

Dieter didn't sleep well that night. He wasn't sure, in fact, that he slept at all. He gave speeches to himself, told himself what he believed, what he stood for, what he was willing to die for. But he also saw images: saw his friend Ernst Gessell, when his body had been torn open; saw Willi Hofmann, with his neck ripped into shreds, remembered the gurgling sounds in his throat. He kept wondering what he would see in the morning. He didn't want to be foolish; Schaefer was not entirely wrong about that. But better to be foolish than spineless. He would rather die than discover that he was a coward.

All was black the next morning, December 16, when the tanks began to roll. Dieter listened to them squeak and rattle as they crawled over the old wooden bridge, an echo reverberating from underneath. The Americans had to hear that. Dieter suspected that the reaction would be almost immediate. But the tanks rolled on and on, dozens of them, and then Dieter's battalion began to move. Two companies marched across the bridge ahead of Dieter's Third Company. But nothing happened, no gunfire, no artillery. Maybe this was going to be easier than Dieter had thought.

By the time Dieter crossed the bridge, daylight was coming on, the gray of heavy clouds showing a haze of light, nothing more. But Dieter was glad to be marching, the movement warming his body and settling his nerves a little. It was another hour before he heard the first sound of battle. Tanks had begun to fire their big guns, and the *zwoop* of mortar fire was in the air. It was all far ahead, however, and it quieted after a time. Dieter's company kept up the hard march.

"The *Amis* must be clearing out. They don't want to face our Tiger Tanks," one of the men said, and some of the others laughed. It was what everyone wanted to believe, and to Dieter it made sense. In Hitler Youth, he had heard it a thousand times. The Americans were not committed to this war. They were in no danger from a war in Europe. Their only real quarrel was with the Japanese, who had attacked them. Besides, Americans were soft people, who had always had life too easy. They would turn and run when they faced a true threat.

Dieter heard a whizzing, windy sound in the air before he heard the pop of the machine gun itself. He stopped dead, looked about, and then suddenly he was on the ground. Schaefer had slammed an arm across his knees and driven him down. But it had all sounded so harmless, like mosquitoes in the air.

What followed was something new. He heard something sucking air—a high-pitched, whooshing sound. He knew only an instant before it hit that he was hearing artillery, close, for the first time in his life. It was up ahead, but when it slammed into the earth, the ground trembled, and then a shock wave rolled over Dieter, slamming into his steel helmet. He ducked his head, held on as the rain of shells continued. There was a fury in it, the shells slamming one after another, the pull of air drawing the breath from his chest. He hadn't been prepared for this; no one had told him how loud it would be, how powerful. For five minutes the ground shook, the air pulsated, and dirt and debris scattered over him. And then it all stopped. But the popping of a machine gun kept up, the whipping noises in the air.

"Schaefer," the squad leader, Sergeant Franke, called, "take the men in your patrol. Work your way around that hill. Get rid of that machine-gun emplacement."

Schaefer cursed softly, but then he said, "All right, follow me. One at a time. Run low, and make it to that brush just beyond the road." Then he turned and said, "Dieter, you go with me. Run when I run."

"I'm all right. I can—"

"You heard me. Run with me. Now!" And then he was up. Dieter jumped up and ran with him. The machine-gun fire was aimed farther up the road, more to the west. Dieter could hear nothing coming his way.

The other three men in the patrol followed, one at a time, and then Schaefer made another run to a place where a wedge of rock jutted out from a hillside. They made two more short runs, and still no fire came their way, but this time Schaefer said, "We crawl now."

Schaefer led out, and he did as he had instructed the others. He stayed flat on his stomach with his rifle resting in the crooks of his arms. He worked his way up the hillside, moving slowly, stopping to listen and watch. There was brush along the side of the hill and little groves of trees. Dieter could still hear the machine gun, but he couldn't see exactly where it was. As he and Schaefer came out from behind a little outcrop of rocks, he finally saw the muzzle fire. It was still a hundred meters ahead, maybe more, toward the top of the hill.

"Fitzmann," Schaefer whispered, "take Berger and go on ahead. We'll move up behind you and be ready to cover if they spot you. Get in as close as you can, and then throw grenades into that emplacement."

The men said nothing. They crawled on ahead. Schaefer moved up, too, but not as fast. He kept watching, ready to provide cover. He and Dieter and the other men had cut the distance in half, however, when Fitzmann and Berger tossed their first grenades. Dieter saw their arms make the flinging motion, saw the long-handled grenades flop through the air, and saw the explosions. He jumped up, ready to cover his men. But Schaefer had hold of Dieter's pant leg, and he jerked him down again. The fire had suddenly turned, was coming their way. Schaefer fired his machine pistol, laying down a hail of bullets, covering for his forward men. And then another grenade hit home, and this one silenced the gun.

Dieter had not yet fired, had forgotten to when the machine-gun fire had come at him. But now he aimed his rifle at the emplacement, and he saw a dark silhouette leap up. One of the Americans was hurrying up the hill behind the gun. Dieter fired, pulled off three quick rounds, and the soldier disappeared. "I shot him, Schaefer. I shot him."

"Be quiet."

Schaefer waited for a time, but then he moved on up the hill, running in short bursts again. When they reached the gun, Fitzmann and Berger were already there. "They're finished," Berger said. "These two are dead. One ran off, but I think he went down, too."

"I shot him," Dieter said. "I got my first American."

No one commented. "Let's get back to our company," Schaefer said. The men walked back down the hill, where Schaefer gave a quick report to the captain, and then the company moved ahead. The rest of the day was mostly quiet after that. The phalanx of soldiers kept driving ahead, straight down the road. The rumor was that the Americans had been routed and were running for their lives.

That night, as the cold deepened, and the men dug into the ground enough to get out of the wind, Dieter was still feeling powerful. He hadn't been frightened. He had done what he had to do, and he had killed an *Ami*—taken his first blood. That was something to remember.

But as things quieted, he found himself less at ease than he wanted to be. A thought kept flitting into his head: Who was the man he had killed? What sort of fellow was he? But that was war, he told himself. He couldn't, absolutely wouldn't, trouble himself about it. He asked Schaefer, "What do you think of my shooting now? I'm not quite as green as you thought?"

"Don't make yourself so important. Not yet. You don't know what it will be like."

"We took some pretty good fire today, and you didn't see me quivering and crying."

"Just be quiet."

"All right, fine. But I will say this. Hitler's made a brilliant move. We're cutting through the Americans like a hot knife through butter."

"Hedrick," Schaefer said, "you haven't seen anything yet, so keep your mouth shut. The Americans have more men, more equipment, more airplanes—more of everything. We caught them by surprise today, but when they get organized, look out."

"What kind of talk is that? Why do you always expect the worst? You should—"

"I told you to be quiet, Hedrick. I mean it."

CHAPTER 8

On December 19, Spence got the word that his division was heading into battle. For several months he had been living at a camp on the Salisbury Plain, west of London. After being pushed through his basic training so fast, he had expected to head straight to the war, but his battalion had been shifted from camp to camp in the United States, and then shipped to England. All through the summer and fall he had continued to train—and all the drills were getting tiresome. The men in his unit wanted to get to the Continent, get in on the action before the war was over. They had missed D-Day, and now they were afraid they would miss the rest.

Spence was part of the recently created 17th Airborne Infantry Division. Rumors had gone around for a long time that the division would be dropped into Germany, behind enemy lines, as the final push to end the war began. But now Hitler had surprised everyone. On the sixteenth he had attacked across the Belgian and Luxembourg borders, and slashed into the Ardennes Forest. The Germans had made good headway those first few days, had made a deep bulge in the American defense lines. "The Battle of the Bulge," newspapers had begun to call the fight in the Ardennes. The 101st and 82nd Airborne divisions had been rushed in to reinforce the battered, retreating American troops. Now the 17th was ready to go.

Spence boarded a C-47 Transport airplane headed for the Continent. The ride was bumpy, and some of the men got sick, but the flight ended with a landing at a field near Reims, in France—away from the action—and not with a parachute drop. After a couple of nights at a camp at Mourmelon, the troops were trucked to a site on the Meuse River, not far from Verdun, where some of the great battles of World War I had been fought. This was only a defensive position—in case the Bulge broke and the Germans drove south into France—and the men of the 17th were disappointed. They wanted to get to the front. They believed in themselves, were hardened and trained; now they wanted to show what they could do. Or at least that's what everyone said. Spence never heard any of the soldiers say much about being afraid, and no one had ever admitted that he hoped the division might sit out the war in England.

What Spence didn't like was sleeping in a foxhole, out

in the cold. The men had dug in in pairs, and Ted Draney and Spence had worked hard on a hole together, getting it deep and roomy. Then they had covered it over with some fir limbs and a couple of shelter halves—the two sides of a pup tent. They hadn't really suffered from the cold those first nights, and Spence had slept fairly well, but he longed for a bed, or at least a cot. There was something not only uncomfortable but a little scary about sleeping in a hole in the ground. He would awaken in the night, unclear for a moment where he was, with the smell of wet earth around him, the damp air touching his face like a cold hand.

On the twenty-fourth of December, snow fell all day, and then, as evening came on, the sky cleared and the temperature dropped like a rock. It was going to be a bitter night. All day, no one had mentioned that it was Christmas Eve—as though the men saw some weakness in bringing up the subject. But as they settled into their foxholes, early, to protect themselves from the cold, someone began to sing "Silent Night." The notes were not really pure, the voice a little too raspy, but the music got into Spence. He had been fighting his feelings all day, trying not to think of home, but the song brought back a whole set of memories: the family get-togethers on Christmas Eve; Dad reading the Christmas story from the Bible; the good food; the excitement about the Christmas morning to follow. Spence never thought of Christmas without remembering the year he had gotten his first bicycle. It had been back in the middle of the Great Depression, and his family had been getting by any way it could. Spence had admitted he wanted a bike, but he hadn't dared to ask for it. Still, on Christmas morning, there it had been, standing up by the Christmas tree, bright red. Spence had seen immediately that the bike was used, that his dad had fixed it up and painted it with a brush, but it hadn't mattered. It had chrome fenders, polished bright, and new tires. Spence was seven at the time, but he had sensed, even then, that he would never in his life be any happier than he was right then.

And he had been right. Spence did remember some other nice times—like the first time LuAnn had agreed to go out with him—but that one morning, on Christmas, when he had gotten his wish, that was as good as anything he had experienced. And his dad had managed it for him; Spence had always understood that. Later, he and his dad hadn't gotten along so well, and Christmas could bring back those memories, too, but that's not what came to him now. He pictured the big table with his relatives from town all sitting around it—uncles and aunts and cousins—and all the food, all the laughing and talking.

The singer, whoever he was, ended his first carol and began "O Come All Ye Faithful." All this time, Spence and Ted hadn't said a word. They were lying next to each other, both in sleeping bags. Almost everything was black around them except for a little opening at one corner in their cover. Through that, Spence could see a thick little patch of stars, and he kept thinking of the nativity scene his mom would put out at Christmastime: the stable and the star overhead.

When Spence had finished his basic training, he had expected to take a trip home. All during those hard times in Georgia he had dreamed of that. He had thought of walking into Dale's, downtown, with his uniform on, and letting the high school kids look at him. He wanted LuAnn to see the man he had become. And he wanted his dad to take him aside and tell him how proud he was that Spence hadn't quit, no matter how hard the training had been.

But all that had never happened. Spence had gotten a seven-day leave, and he had expected to grab the first train out of town, headed west. He knew he had to allow two days each way, but that would still give him three days at home. The only trouble was, the trains were moving troops, and most of them were full. He couldn't get on one. Then, when he tried to buy a bus ticket, he found that he couldn't get anything for a couple of days, and that wouldn't leave him enough time to do any more than arrive, turn around, and head back. So he had been stuck at Fort Benning with nothing to do but think about home. What he knew now was that the next time he saw

Brigham City would probably be at the end of the war—and who knew how long that might be?

Ted finally asked, "Are you awake?"

"Sure."

"Are you homesick?"

"A little, maybe."

"Yeah. Me too. Everyone is, I'd guess."

"Sure."

"I sort of wish we'd move up tomorrow and get into this thing," Ted said. "I don't like all this sitting around and waiting."

"I know."

They listened again, until the song ended, and then came the next one: "It Came Upon a Midnight Clear."

At home, the Sunday school had always put on a Christmas pageant. When Spence was a kid, he would play a shepherd. He would pose near the manger in his bathrobe, with a dishcloth wrapped around his head and draped down his back. He had hated the whole business as he had gotten to be ten or eleven and was still too short ever to be chosen to play Joseph, but when he was finally old enough to sit in the congregation, he had been able to laugh at his little brother, dressed in the same funny getup and sneaking little waves to his family. Spence wondered how much Lloyd had changed in the last year, wished that he could see him for a few minutes. Lloyd was thirteen now, nearing fourteen, and Mom had written that he had grown half a foot since Spence had left. He was already five seven, an inch taller than Spence, and he seemed to be a better ballplayer. Spence wished he could get back home for a furlough or something, just once to see Lloyd and Evelyn and Betty before they had grown up too much. Louise was going with a boy named Sterling Carter, from up in Honeyville. He was home from the war with a bad knee, shot up in a battle on the little island of Biak, in the Pacific. Mom said she thought he and Louise were getting pretty serious. Spence figured they would probably be married before he saw Louise again.

Since the end of basic training, Spence had been through some lonely months. He had never really become much a part of his company. Most of the men were older and used to different ways. Spence had stuck to his promise not to drink or smoke, but that had cut him off from almost everyone. He had learned not to accept invitations when the guys in his squad headed into town. It was not just that they got drunk and got into fights; they also headed straight to any whorehouse they could find. No one else seemed to believe that God was watching, knew what a person did; but for Spence, that idea was basic to the way he looked at life. Going to a prostitute was worse than almost anything, and he knew he could never go home and marry a nice girl, not if he had done that.

At least Ted wasn't so different. Ted had chewed tobacco some, before joining up, and he had taken up smoking the way most of the boys had. But he didn't drink much at all, and he always bragged that he was never going to "pay for it," when the men asked him to go along to the brothels. But that was just Ted's way of sounding tough. Spence knew that his Baptist upbringing was part of what kept him out of those places.

The only trouble was, Spence and Ted took some hard ribbing from the other men. They were two of the youngest, and that was bad enough, but some of the men never let up on them for being such "Sunday school" boys. Vic Barela had told them, "When the fighting starts, I hate to think what these two boys are going to do. Fill their pants, probably."

Ted was the one more likely to say, "Don't worry. We'll hold our own. Just make sure you do the same." And Ted had once even taken a guy on, fought him nose to nose, and come out about even with him. But Spence's reaction was to withdraw. At times he had the feeling that some of the men liked him, saw him as some sort of little brother, but that didn't mean they ever got off his back, and he was tired of it. He was tired of all the hard talking, too, the cursing and talking dirty. He'd heard all that before, and he tried not to worry about it, but some guys never knew when to quit.

Ted talked a little more than Spence did, and he was taller and bigger built, but just like Spence, he was from a little town and he had farmed all his life. He came from a big family, too—seven or eight kids. Spence could never keep track of all the names. But mostly Ted talked about his brother, just younger, the way Spence talked about Lloyd. This brother—his name was Kenny—wrote funny letters, telling all about high school and his little hometown, Idalia, Colorado, and what the people did there. Ted would read the letters out loud and he would laugh until he'd have to stop, and then he'd tell about all the people who lived in his town.

Spence also liked Sergeant Pappas, the little man who led the squad. He was a no-nonsense guy, who had fought with the 101st Airborne on D-Day, and then had gotten himself wounded in Holland. He thought a squad ought to be a unit, so he tried to stop the razzing when it got too strong.

"Do you wonder what it will be like when we get up to the front?" Ted asked.

Spence was taken a little by surprise. Sometimes he had wanted to bring the subject up, but it had always been Ted who had stayed away from it. "Yeah. Sure, I do." But then he added, "But we'll get through all right, I guess."

"Some of them guys, they make it sound like they're not scared of anything."

"That's just big talk. Everybody's at least a little scared now."

Another song had started: "O Little Town of

Bethlehem." The guy singing was warming up, getting better all the time. His voice seemed the only thing out there in the air now, cleaner than before, and penetrating, as though it were coming right through the earth around them. "No ear may hear his coming; but in this world of sin, where meek souls will receive him, still, the dear Christ enters in." Spence had never thought of the words much before, wasn't even sure he knew what they meant. But he longed for something: some comfort the language seemed to suggest, some feeling he remembered from home, at Christmas. He could feel his throat tighten, his chest beginning to quiver.

"We didn't even have to join when we did," Ted said. "We could have waited another year."

"We would have gone in, anyway. We've still got Japan to fight."

"I know. But sometimes I wish I had this last year back. There's all kinds of things I've never done yet."

"We'll be all right, Ted. We'll do all that stuff later on. It's not good to start thinking about things like that." But Spence *had* been thinking about it, and now he was holding his breath. He would feel like such a baby if he started to bawl.

"We've got to turn the Germans around," Ted said, "and then we have to get through that Siegfried Line and across the Rhine. It's going to be bad, Spence. Every bit of it's going to be really bad."

"I know." Spence took a good, deep breath, and then he said, "But we knew that coming in."

"No, we didn't. Not really. Not the way we know it now."

"We know more than we did."

Spence knew what Ted meant, of course: that the war was finally close enough to feel. But he still wondered what would happen inside him when he faced the fire.

"I wish that guy would shut up," Ted said. "He shouldn't be singing all them songs."

But Spence didn't feel that way. He wanted to hear the words one more time: "No ear may hear his coming." He liked the thought of that, liked to think that "the dear Christ" was with him now.

Christmas Day was not quite as bad as Spence expected. For one thing, the cooks were all set up with a good field kitchen, and though the Christmas dinner wasn't exactly like the one at home, it was pretty good. The men seemed to lay off a little that day too. Most of them were friendly—maybe thinking about Christmas, or maybe thinking about going into battle.

That afternoon, mail arrived—mail that was just catching up from England. That was a boost. Spence had three letters: two from his parents, and one from his sister Louise. He opened them in the order they had been posted, and he enjoyed all the news: Christmas preparations, Lloyd playing basketball on the freshman team, and all the rest. But the second letter from his parents brought the news he had expected for a while: LuAnn had gotten engaged to Dennis Stevens.

Spence hadn't held out any hope of ever having her. It wasn't that. But it was one step closer to what he had dreaded for a long time. And it had come at a bad time.

CHAPTER 9

Dieter's company made another push forward on Christmas Day. Dieter didn't know exactly where they were, but he had seen a road sign that said, BASTOGNE, 14 KILOMETERS, and someone in the company said that Bastogne was in Belgium, not Luxembourg. "From what I'm hearing, the Americans are dug in there, and they're hanging on," Schaefer told Dieter. "It's a crossroads for this area, and they can slow down our offensive, maybe even stop it, if they can hold on to it."

"Then why don't we take it? Why did we stop so soon today?" It was late in the day, and Dieter was surprised at how little ground they were taking now. The first few days had been like a pleasure walk, and then everything had slowed, and now the crash of artillery was constant up ahead.

"We moved as far as we could. The companies up front took a beating all day. You heard the artillery."

"But we have better tanks. Why don't we smash our way straight into Bastogne—and rout the *Amis*, the way our commander said we would?"

"They're dug in, and we're on the move. That makes us easy targets."

"That's an excuse, Schaefer. Good soldiers don't make excuses."

Schaefer and Dieter had scraped away the snow from the ground, but now they were trying to crack through the frozen earth with their little entrenching shovels. The weather had turned much worse. Snow had fallen the day before, and after the storm the temperature had dropped. Schaefer rested for a moment, took some deep breaths. "Hedrick, we've been in reserve, so far—following the lead companies. You don't know what it's like to be at the front. One of these days they'll send us up and let those guys fall back. When that happens, we'll see how you talk."

"I look forward to that day, Schaefer."

"Yes, yes. No doubt." Schaefer laughed a little, and then began hacking at the ground again.

Dieter wasn't going to argue about such things with Schaefer. It was pointless. He remembered how he had felt that first morning when artillery had started to strike nearby and machine guns were firing. He could admit to himself now that he had been afraid. But heroes weren't people who were unafraid. Heroes were people who did what they had to do, afraid or not.

It took Dieter and Corporal Schaefer most of the evening to dig an adequate foxhole. But the work kept them busy and kept them warm. They were wearing their heavy winter gear, white for camouflage, and for a time Dieter got warm enough to throw off his coat. But when they finally got the hole deep enough, and got in, their bodies cooled quickly. Inside the heavy clothes, Dieter could feel his sweat turning cold, and he wondered whether it would freeze in his clothes, against his body. He hated the nights, so miserably cold, and sleep so difficult. Schaefer was drifting off into one of his silent moods again, and that meant nothing to do but sit there, or try to sleep, and the night would last forever. This time of year, it seemed as though the sun hardly came up before it set again.

There was something on Dieter's mind, too. He had been fighting off the thoughts all day, but they kept working their way into his consciousness. It was Christmas Day, even though the men all seemed to go out of their way not to mention it. He kept thinking about his home, his farm. His family had always celebrated for three full days: Christmas Eve, Christmas Day, and the "Second Day of Christmas," on the twenty-sixth. That was a day for another fine dinner and more visits from relatives. The three days lived in Dieter's mind as a brightness in the dark of winter—the cold held out by the fire inside, all the laughter. And always, he had gone to mass with his family. His Hitler Youth leaders had derided religion and taught that it led people into a stupid sentimentality that good Nazi party members couldn't afford. Maybe that was true. Dieter didn't know what he believed about God and all the things his parents believed, but he did think fondly on the Christmas Eve mass, the music, the festive decorations. This dark Christmas night was the first for him, away from his family and all that light. In the silence, now, with Schaefer off in his own thoughts, Dieter finally allowed himself to picture his parents, to ask himself what everyone back home was doing. He promised himself that he would only allot a little time for that, and then he would turn his thoughts to something else.

But Schaefer said, "This is your first Christmas away from home, isn't it?"

"Yes. Certainly," Dieter said, and he tried to sound matter-of-fact.

"I've been gone four times now. The last time I was home for Christmas was nineteen forty."

"I thought you went home after you were wounded."

"I did. But not until August. And then I was sent out here. Last Christmas I was in a hospital, in Poland. That wasn't so bad."

"We'll have plenty of time for Christmas after we win this war."

"Just be quiet if that's all you can say, Hedrick. I don't want to listen to any of that tonight." Schaefer leaned back and was quiet for a time, but then he startled Dieter by beginning to sing. *"Stille Nacht, Heilige Nacht."* His voice was hoarse, ugly, but he could carry a tune better than Dieter would have thought, and he sang the song all the way through, every verse, every word.

Dieter felt it all, but he didn't protest.

"You sing one," Schaefer said, when he was finished.

"No. I can't sing."

"What song do you like?"

"It doesn't matter."

"No. Tell me."

"I don't know. *'O du Fröliche,'* I suppose."

"Yes. Everyone likes that one." And Schaefer sang it through. "Oh you happy, oh you blessed, grace-bringing Christmas day. The world was lost, Christ was born; take joy, all Christianity."

Dieter listened, but when Schaefer was finished, he felt the need to say something, to prove that he was in control of his emotions. "So tell me, Corporal, do you believe in God, then?"

"No. I guess not."

"Why sing such things, then?"

"I like the songs. I like the memories."

"Then why no faith in God?"

"I don't know. I thought I believed right up until the

moment I knew I didn't. Suddenly, nothing was there. I wanted to pray, but the idea was stupid to me, and I couldn't do it."

"What happened?" Dieter was still trying to sound as though he were merely chatting, but he was a little afraid of what Schaefer might say.

"I got a letter from my wife. I was on the eastern front, near Stalingrad, and it was the heart of winter. We had had no mail for a long time, and we were in the worst conditions you can imagine. Men were starving to death, freezing to death. Finally, we got a little food, and we got our mail. I opened my letters—four or five of them—and in one, months old, was the news that my son had been killed."

"Killed in action?"

"Yes. In a way. He was in Hitler Youth, like you, and he was manning an antiaircraft gun, near Mannheim, where I'm from. He was only seventeen. The last time I had seen him, he had been fourteen. Just a boy—happy, a good football player, innocent of everything."

"He died for his country, Schaefer. You have that to be proud of." Dieter knew when he said the words that they would bother Schaefer, but it was the truth, what the man should think.

Schaefer took a long breath, and then muttered, "I can't talk to you. I simply can't do it."

Dieter knew better than to say anything else, and

actually, he was sorry—not for what he had said, but merely that he had said it, knowing how Schaefer thought about things. But the man was a sad case, someone who had lost his will.

"Do you have any idea how many boys have died in this war, Hedrick? German boys? Russian boys? American and English boys? Chinese? Japanese? Polish? Canadian? Australian? How many little children? How many women?"

"The Americans and Brits are swine, Schaefer. They're the ones who attack civilians."

"Do you think that *we* don't?"

"We bomb London, in retaliation, but they are the ones who—"

"You believe all these lies. You know nothing. We attacked London early on, in the beginning. We wiped out Warsaw. We're as much to blame as anyone for all this killing of children and women and little boys."

That couldn't be true. Dieter was sure it wasn't, but he wouldn't argue with this man. He would only pity him. The man had lost a son, and that was something Dieter could try to understand.

"Dieter, there's something I want to tell you. You won't believe me, but listen, anyway, and the time might come when you'll see that I'm right."

Schaefer almost never called him Dieter, rarely spoke with such gentleness. The tone only frightened Dieter.

"Save your words, Schaefer," he said. "I won't listen to you. I won't ever believe the distortions I hear from you."

"You'll listen because you can't do otherwise." But then he hesitated before he said, "You need to know this. We aren't moving fast enough. The Americans retreated for a while, but now they're holding, and that means we've lost this battle. The Americans and British have troops all over France and Holland. They're all rushing here now. You can bet on that. Once they hit us with all they've got, we're dead. We'll have to retreat back into Germany—that or be taken prisoner. Or die."

"Then I'll die first."

"If that's what you want, you'll have the chance. Plenty will. But that's what I want to tell you. Don't do it, Dieter. Don't do it. Go back to your parents. Don't break their hearts."

"I don't want to hear this, Schaefer. I told you that. It's more traitorous talk. I could have you shot for the things you've said to me."

"Just listen to me. I have some good advice for you. You'll claim to refuse it, but remember it when the time comes."

Dieter decided to be silent, to let Schaefer talk, but not to let the ideas sink in.

"First, if we get overrun, and you get the chance, surrender. That's your best chance of surviving this war."

"Swine."

"Second, if I get wounded or killed, find one of the older men to partner with. They've learned how to stay alive, and you haven't."

"Schweinhund."

"Listen to me, Dieter. You didn't answer my question before. But I know this. Millions of boys are dying in this war. Millions. The only thing you should care about now is staying alive. Germany has already lost the war. The Russians have won in the east. And now the enemy are overtaking us in the west. This battle is desperate, just a wild gamble, and it isn't going to work. So there's nothing left to fight for. Save your own life. Don't die for that pig Hitler."

But this was too much, "You can't say that to me," Dieter shouted, and suddenly he lunged at Schaefer, swung his fist at the voice. But he hit the man's big coat in the chest or shoulder, and then Schaefer grabbed Dieter's wrist and held it. Dieter tried the other fist this time, and got in a punch at Schaefer's face, but it didn't seem to move the man, and now he had hold of both Dieter's wrists. And the sickening man was saying softly, "It's all right, son. I don't blame you. But I'm telling you the truth. I beg you, don't get yourself killed. It isn't worth it."

Dieter struggled a little against Schaefer's grip, but not much. He didn't have the strength to break free.

CHAPTER 10

On the day after Christmas, Spence's battalion boarded trucks and moved north, closer to the front. The truck drivers dropped the men off, threw off some equipment, and got out fast, but Spence saw no sign of any action nearby. In the distance he heard rumblings of artillery fire, and down the hill from where he was standing he could see two burned-out American Sherman tanks and a German *Panzer*. "That looks like one of those big Tiger Tanks," Ted said.

Spence nodded, but what he had noticed now were some dark lumps alongside the German tank. He was pretty sure they were bodies.

"Hey, look at that," Vic Barela said. "Stiffs. I'm going down there to check 'em out. Maybe I can pick me up some souvenirs."

But Sergeant Pappas said, "Just stay where you are.

We've got to find out where we're digging in."

So the men stood where they had been dropped off—and waited—but the feeling was eerie. What if they were being watched by the enemy? Maybe Germans were zeroing in with their artillery already. "Shouldn't we take cover somewhere?" Spence asked Ted.

"I don't know. I guess the officers know what they're doing."

"I wonder."

But it wasn't long until the entire company was marched off to a nearby woods. Each platoon was assigned an area along the edge of the trees, and then each squad was placed by the platoon leader, but it was Sergeant Pappas who picked a spot for Spence and Ted. "Dig in right here," he told them. "This is the perimeter we have to hold. The ground under all this snow is frozen harder 'n rock, I'm sure, so start digging if you want to sleep warm tonight."

"Sleep warm. Right," Spence muttered, and Ted laughed. But they began to scrape the crusted snow away, and then for the next couple hours they dug into the frozen ground. The sergeant came by once and told them, "When artillery hits in these trees, it sends broken limbs flying—just like harpoons. Those things can stab right through you. So cover your holes and stay close. As soon as the Krauts realize we're here, they'll want to give us something to think about."

"Where are we, anyway?" Spence asked.

"They don't tell me nothing like that. All I know is that we're in Belgium. And someone said a town called Bastogne is over that way." He pointed in a direction that Spence figured was mostly east. "That's where the 101st got tied up. They've been surrounded, is what I heard on the radio. Patton is supposed to be marching the Third Army in there from the south, but I haven't heard anything about whether he got there or not."

"What about the Germans? Do we know where they are?"

"Somebody does. I don't."

"Wouldn't it be easier if we knew what was going on?"

"The big boys tell me that if we don't know nothing, we can't tell the Krauts nothing, either—if we get taken prisoner. So I guess that's about right."

None of this seemed like the stuff Spence had seen in the movies. How could they be in a war and not know what they were doing?

"I'll tell you this much," Pappas said. "I'd dig that hole good, but I got a feeling we might be here just for tonight, and then move up some more tomorrow or the next day. I'm just basing that on some things the lieutenant said."

"You gotta be joking," Ted told him. "We could be digging another hole like this tomorrow?"

"I didn't say I know that for sure. But if they move us again, don't complain to me."

What Spence knew was that the sergeant—a Greek kid from New Jersey, maybe twenty-two or twenty-three—had at least seen some action, knew the ropes some. And he was one of very few in their company who did.

Night came early, and by then Spence was glad that he and Ted had worked hard on their foxhole. The day had been a little warmer than the days before, but once the sun went down, it didn't take long to know that the night was going to be brutal. Ted and Spence got into their sleeping bags with their coats on, their boots, but the cold still penetrated. Spence couldn't imagine that he would get any sleep. "Do you think we'll see some action tomorrow?" he finally asked.

"I wouldn't be surprised." All the training, all this time going by, and now the shooting was finally going to start. The idea made Spence nervous.

"Spence, I know you're religious, but how come you never say much about it?"

"I don't know. You don't, either."

"I know." For a time there was only breathing, and then Ted said, "I always went to church, but I never thought much about it. You know what I mean?"

"That's how I was too. Lately, though, I've been thinking more about everything."

"Yeah. Same here. My preacher got me aside before I left, and he told me not to get all full of hate. He said if I'm a real Christian, I ought to love my enemy. I told him I didn't know how a guy was supposed to do that. But I got to thinking the other day—you know, on Christmas—my problem is, I don't think I hate enough. I think out here, you need to hate. That's the only way to do this."

"I haven't thought near enough about any of that stuff," Spence said. "My dad told me I ought to be a good example to other guys, and all like that, but I don't have enough worked out in my own head."

"You're a good example to me."

"But I need more inside of me, like my dad and my big brother. Robert wanted to kill Japs, but he was plenty religious. I guess a guy can do both."

"I don't know. But I think I'd rather hate the Krauts if I'm going to kill 'em."

"I'll tell you what I keep thinking. I know this sounds stupid—it's not like everyone doesn't know it already— but it just seems like we shouldn't have wars."

"That's what I've been thinking. I guess we're a couple of geniuses, aren't we?"

The boys laughed, and Spence was a little embarrassed, but it's what he did feel. At home, he'd wanted so much to get to the war and let everyone know what kind of a man he was. He'd wanted to wear his pants tucked into his boots, to jump out of airplanes, to be brave, but he hadn't thought enough about what he would be doing when he finally got to the battle. Maybe tomorrow he would kill someone, and he wasn't sure how he was going to feel about that.

The boys huddled together, and they managed to sleep at times, but the night lasted so long that sometimes Spence wondered whether he hadn't missed a day, whether they hadn't stayed in their holes all day and started another night.

When morning finally did come, Spence and Ted stayed down out of the wind, and only moved back their cover enough to look out a little. Sergeant Pappas came by and said, "No fires. Eat what you can, and then we're moving out."

"Oh, brother," Ted mumbled. Both the boys stood up and looked out of their hole into the brightness of all the snow.

"Hey, I told you that's what would probably happen."

"Where we going?"

"That way. That's all I know." The sergeant pointed down the hill into a long, open valley. In the bottom were the damaged tanks, the bodies, but otherwise, everything was beautiful. On the hillsides, north of the valley, was a little forest of fir trees, black against the snow, and the rest of the valley was white and glistening, pure. Spence had to wonder, where was this war everyone was talking about?

Spence opened cans of cold SPAM, hard biscuits, and fruit cocktail frozen solid in his pack. He hated all of it, but he was hungry and he knew he would need his strength today. The truth was, even though he had to dig a new hole that night, he was thankful not to be sitting around. The hike through the snow would warm him up, and it was hard to think that anything very dangerous lay ahead in this peaceful valley.

When the men finally pushed off, Sergeant Pappas told them to walk in double file along both sides of a little road, to spread out and leave plenty of space between each other. "You bunch up and one 88 shell could knock you all out."

Maybe so, but spreading out that way made for a lonely hike. And when Spence marched past those bodies—three frozen Germans, their faces blue as ice, their eyes rigid—he was left with a strange feeling. One of the Germans looked young, maybe his own age. He was lying on his back, his legs bent under him, exactly as he had fallen. Barela shouted from behind, "Hey, the master race dies the same as the rest of us—when you put a bullet in 'em."

But Spence was still struck with how normal the kid had looked, like lots of guys he knew back home. He found himself wondering who the boy was.

The company marched all morning, sat and ate something from K-ration cans, and then moved out again. The walk was hard, and men traded off, taking the lead through the snow. But Spence liked this much better than the dark hours. He just hoped they stopped soon, so they could start digging early enough to be ready for the night.

And then someone screamed, "Shell!" Spence dove

to the ground on his face in the snow. He had heard the sound, too, and hadn't known what is was for a moment. It came as a hissing sound, a high-pitched shriek followed by a deep whoosh just before the explosion. Spence felt the earth shake, and then a burst of whining, spinning sounds screamed over him. At the same time another shell hit, and he heard the same whirling, whistling again. By then he knew it was shrapnel in the air. He dug at the snow, tried to get flatter, lower. A third shell struck, even closer, and someone screamed, "I'm hit! I'm hit! Help me!" The panic in the soldier's voice was wild, hardly human, and it froze Spence in place.

"Help me! Help me! Please!"

Spence didn't look up. His face was in the snow, his hands over his head pulling his helmet down to cover his forehead. The better part of a minute passed, and then the sound was in the air again. Three more shells hit in quick succession, closer to Spence. He felt the concussion hammer him, pull at him, suck the air from his lungs. He knew he was supposed to keep his mouth open, to protect his ears, but his jaw was clenched, his muscles locked.

More men were screaming. "Oh, Mama, Mama, help me," someone close to Spence was moaning. Spence tried to think what he could do for the man, but he couldn't get himself to move. His impulse was to dig deeper, get lower, but his muscles wouldn't do that, either.

From somewhere distant, Spence heard a muffled

voice. "You've got to move those men. They'll all die out there in the open."

And then Sergeant Pappas was screaming, "Let's go! Head for the trees off to your right! On the double!"

It was only the rage in the sergeant's voice that propelled Spence. He came up suddenly and took off hard, and he didn't worry about anyone else. He ran for the trees, all out, fought his way through the snow. And when the next set of three explosions struck, he didn't dive back to the ground the way some did. He just wanted cover, deep cover, and so he kept going. He dove into some brush next to a tree, his lungs stinging with pain and his body trembling, but he had no sooner covered up, felt hidden, than he realized that if artillery struck in these trees, he could be in worse trouble. Why had his leaders sent him here?

"Move on through," someone was yelling. "We can't get caught in these woods. We need to get to the other side where those gun crews can't see us."

Spence jumped up and ran again, slogged through the snow, ran like someone was right behind, chasing him. He was out on the other side of the woods in just a few minutes, but then he didn't know what to do. His impulse was to keep running—in any direction.

"Okay, everyone. Calm down," a lieutenant was saying. "Stop here. Those guys on that gun can't see us now. They won't waste shells until they find out where we are.

Get back into the edge of the woods here until I find out where we're going to have you dig in."

Spence didn't know who the officer was, what company he was from. He also had no idea what had happened to Ted. Maybe he was down somewhere, shot up with shrapnel. Spence began to feel ashamed. The first time he had faced danger he had run like a little kid. He hadn't even tried to look out for his buddy. What kind of a soldier was he going to be? But he was still shaking, still terrorized by the sound of that shrapnel spinning over his head, men screeching like gut-shot animals.

When Spence looked around, he could see that everyone else was just as shaken as he was. They were all bunched up close, but no one spoke, no one even made eye contact. After a time, Ted finally came up through the trees, and he seemed relieved to spot Spence. "You all right?" he asked.

"Sure."

"That was bad. I didn't know it would be like that."

Spence nodded.

It was almost dark when the men finally moved out. By then they were reorganized, back with their squads. Sergeant Pappas led his men to another little grove of trees, a little farther along the ridge overlooking the valley. "Okay, men, you gotta dig in again, along this tree line," he told them. "I wish I could tell you we'll be here again tomorrow night, but I can't say for sure."

Spence wanted to get down as deep in the ground as he could, and he wanted to stay there. So he and Ted worked hard. After half an hour or so, deep in the dark, and hardly able to tell what they were doing, Spence heard the sound again, and this time he knew instantly. He and Ted dropped into the hole, but it wasn't a foot deep yet. If a shell hit close and blew up trees around them, they were dead. But something new was going on. These shells were coming like rain, a barrage. A wild sort of howling, like a siren, constant and intense, filled the woods, and with it, the crashing, whizzing, whining. Spence kept sucking for air, but couldn't breathe. The earth rolled, seemed to jump under him at times, and the concussions slapped him back and forth. And then a limb crashed onto the boys. But they hadn't taken a hit, and the limb seemed like a kind of protection.

All of it lasted only a few minutes, but when the noise stopped, Spence was weak. "What was that?" he asked Ted.

"I don't know."

"It was like a hundred guns going off. I don't know how they could shoot that many shells."

In a few minutes, Sergeant Pappas came through the trees, whispering, "Morgan, Draney, is that you?"

"Yeah."

"Are you two all right?"

"Yeah. I guess. What was that?"

"It's what we call a Screamy Meemie. It's some kind of multibarreled thing. The Germans call it a fog-thrower."

"Anyone hit?"

"Yeah."

"How bad?"

"Lassiter and Jones took a direct hit. There's nothing left of them."

"What do you mean?" Spence asked. He knew it was a stupid question, but he just couldn't believe what the sergeant had said. Lassiter and Jones had gone all the way through basic with him. They couldn't be dead already, the very first day they'd seen action.

"Just what I said. Bigler got it too, this afternoon, when those first shells came in. He's not dead, but he's in bad shape."

"Is he going to make it?"

"I don't know. He took a piece of shrapnel in the back, and another one tore his jaw most of the way off." There was silence for a moment, and Pappas seemed to realize he was telling these boys the wrong things. "But listen, dig in deep and you'll be all right. I've got to check the rest of the men. Get yourself a good hole dug before they fire that thing at us again."

"Okay."

Spence dug hard, hammering away at the ground with his entrenching tool, and when he got into softer soil he shoveled as though he were trying to dig a well.

He didn't understand any of this. He had seen war in his head so many times, imagined it, but this was all wrong. It was digging and waiting, with guns miles away blowing people up. How was he supposed to be brave against something too big, too far off, to face and fight?

"This is a mess," he told Ted. "This is a crazy mess. We're going to get ourselves blown into pieces one of these days if things keep up like this."

"I don't know where we are," Ted said. "And I don't know where those guns are."

It was the same thing Spence had been thinking. "We need some airplanes. We can't fight tanks and guns with rifles."

Spence was angry. Why hadn't anyone told him, just once, what it was really going to be like out here?

"Lassiter and Jones are dead," he told Ted. He was still trying to get it through his head.

"I was talking to those guys coming through the woods on the way over here," Ted said. "Jones was complaining about digging holes all the time."

"I gave Lassiter the cigarettes from my K-ration box. Traded him for Hershey bars."

Ted stopped digging. Spence could hear him taking long breaths. "Jones had a girl waiting for him," he finally said. "He was engaged to her, I think."

Spence had seen the girl's picture. She was no movie star—just a girl with kind of a nice smile. Fairly pretty.

One of these days she was going to get the news. So were Jones's parents. He had little brothers and sisters, too. He had shown Spence a family picture.

"It sounds like Bigler's in bad shape."

But that was worse to think about—a boy's jaw torn loose, steel in his back. "Let's not talk about it," Spence said. "Let's just get this hole dug."

CHAPTER II

Spence and Ted put in another hard night. At some point in the endless darkness, Spence realized that his toes were freezing. "You asleep?" he asked Ted.

"I don't know. Not exactly."

That was about right, Spence thought. "I think my feet are freezing up," he told Ted.

"We're supposed to take our boots off and rub them."

"I know. That's the last thing I want to do, but I guess I'd better do it." Spence had seen the films on foot care, on trench foot and frostbite, and he knew a guy could lose his toes pretty fast. He sat up and, without getting out of his sleeping bag, tried to work one of his boots off. It was a tight enough squeeze for two of them down there together, but pulling the stiff boot off was a hard job. "What about your feet?" he asked Ted.

"I don't know. They don't hurt much, but they've been numb for three days."

"We gotta get your boots off, too." Part of what Spence liked was something to do, some excuse to move. He was sick of waiting out these nights. After working so hard all day, he felt as though he ought to sleep soundly, but fear had become a third partner, felt like it was snuggled up with him. He hated this tight little hole, and he longed for light, but he didn't want to get out, either. Out in the open, danger had room to maneuver, to come at them from any direction.

Spence got one boot off, finally, and his sock, which had gotten wet and was frozen.

"Put the sock inside your shirt, next to your body," Ted told him. "It's the best way to dry anything. At least that's what they told us in survival training."

"Best way to freeze my ribs solid," Spence said, but he unbuttoned his coat, unzipped his field jacket, unbuttoned his shirt, and worked the sock inside on top of his long underwear. Everything was such a chore. In a minute he would have to dig though his pockets and find his change of socks, but his hands were freezing and so was that bare foot. When he began to rub his toes, pain shot through his foot, like bee stings.

"What's the matter?" Ted asked, obviously hearing Spence moan.

"My toes are like ice. It hurts to move 'em."

"It's supposed to hurt when the blood starts to circulate. Here—let me help you." Spence didn't know what Ted had in mind, but he was sitting up, twisting around. "Get your foot up here and I'll stick it inside my coat for a few minutes. That'll thaw it out faster than anything."

Spence worked his leg out of the sleeping bag, turned around, and then slid back so he could stick his foot toward Ted. As it turned out, the heat under Ted's arm, along his side, was welcome, but painful, as his foot came to life. Spence knew this was what they had been taught to do, but it still embarrassed him a little. He was sort of glad for the dark.

"Did your mom ever heat up a rock, or something like that, and put it in the foot of your bed?" Ted asked.

"No. Not that I remember. I've heard about my parents doing that, though, staying warm in a buggy that way."

"We didn't have electricity out on our farm," Ted said, "not until I was ten or eleven. The whole house was heated by a coal stove in the kitchen. It was just a little house, but the bedrooms would get cold as all get out. Mom would pile up a bunch of quilts, and then she'd heat up a big round rock in the oven and stick it in the bed—wrapped in a towel or something—before me and my brother would run and jump in. I'll tell you, that rock felt awful good."

"What did you do in the evenings, in the winter, without electricity?"

"My mom and dad don't have much education, but both of 'em like to read. We read a lot of books together, and played checkers, stuff like that. Then in the summer, me and Kenny stayed outside just as long as we could. We'd catch frogs, down at the pond. Bugs, water snakes—anything. We killed some big old rattlesnakes, too. We ran pretty wild, I guess, but we sure do have a lot of good memories."

"Me and Lloyd were kind of like that—except Dad worked us quite a bit."

"Yeah, well, we worked, too. But Kenny always figured out a way to have a good time. Even if he worked, it seemed like we were playing a game. I remember one time he wanted to drive dad's tractor, and he didn't really know how. He got it going and didn't know what to do—ran it into the side of our chicken coop and knocked a big hole in the side. Dad tried to be mad, but Kenny got him laughing about it."

"He sounds a little like Lloyd. That kid is always fouling something up, but it never worries him too much. He got away with all kinds of things that Dad wouldn't let me and Robert do."

"Yup. Same thing."

Spence felt the warmth sinking into his foot, and he wasn't quite so self-conscious about it the more they just talked. Eventually, he got a dry sock on the foot, and his boot back on, and then he pulled his other boot off. Ted warmed that one, too, the same way, and they talked some more about their families, about teasing sisters, mostly, tricks they had pulled. Then Spence took his turn, took Ted's bare feet, one at a time, in against his own body. It all took time, which was good, and when the two finally tried to sleep again, Spence was glad for the dry feel of his new socks, even if his feet were aching worse than before. But he was also full of thoughts about Lloyd, about the two of them teasing Louise, about the time they had traded a bushel of Dad's Bing cherries for a basketball and then got caught for it. And he thought about Ted, how much fun they might have had if they had grown up in Brigham City together.

Spence did manage to get a little sleep. It was still early, however, when Sergeant Pappas came to the fox-hole and said, "Morgan, Draney, eat something. As soon as first light breaks, we're going to clear the woods just down the valley from here."

"All right, Sergeant," Ted said, and then the two went through another complicated procedure: finding cans of K-rations in the dark, opening them with their bayonets, eating whatever happened to be inside whether it was what they had hoped or not. Spence ended up with some Vienna sausages, which weren't too bad, so he split those with Ted. He also found some cheese and some dry biscuits, but there was nothing to drink since the water in their canteens was frozen.

When they finally pulled themselves out of the hole, Spence realized the worst: that he needed to relieve himself, needed to pull his pants down. He didn't dare go far off, but he slipped a few steps into the darkness, and fortunately Ted had found some toilet paper in his pack. Spence had never gotten used to the inconvenience of living this way. The time with his pants down, bent over a log, was not just cold but was awkward, with so much gear hanging off him. He thought of mornings back home when he had complained that his sister had taken too long in the bathroom. What he wouldn't have given now for the light, the heat, the mirror, the soap and water he always had at home.

Other men were taking care of the same needs, and plenty of grumbling was going on. The sergeant kept whispering for everyone to keep the noise down. Finally, he led the squad to an assembly point, where Lieutenant Nowland, the platoon leader, whispered instructions. "Just as soon as we can see a little more, we're going to fan out in a skirmish line. We're going to work our way through the woods down this valley a little way. But here's the problem. These Europeans replant their forests after they cut them. Once you get twenty or thirty feet in, you won't be able to see each other most of the time. The trees are all the same size, and they're in rows, so they all look exactly alike. It's easy to get lost. Keep moving forward, and check your compasses once in a while, but don't start shooting each other. We know we've got Krauts up ahead, in a little village, but we don't know what to expect in the woods. So go easy, watch what you're doing, and don't shoot unless you know what you're shooting at."

This didn't sound good at all. Spence glanced at Ted. "Let's stay within sight of each other," Ted whispered. That did sound like a good idea. But when the sergeant got them set up to go, he had them spread farther apart than Spence had expected. Just as Nowland had warned, once into the trees, it was not only hard to see anyone left or right, it was hard to know directions. In the early gray light, the trees, all firs, were like giant watchmen, and each one could have been hiding a sniper or even a machine-gun emplacement. Spence kept moving ahead, sinking deep into the snow, each step, and then jerking his foot back up, high, to take another stride ahead. He liked the warmth he felt in his body, but he hated everything else—the loneliness, the fear of what might be hiding behind the next tree, the work of moving ahead in the snow.

The walking took his full power, full attention, and after maybe fifteen minutes he was not very confident he was heading in the right direction or that he was out there with anyone else. He checked his compass as he took a breather, and then whispered, "Ted," but he got no answer. The snow on the trees muffled the sounds. What he wanted to do, more than anything, was to bolt to his right and yell for Ted or for his sergeant. It was all he could do to keep moving ahead.

What he found, after a time, however, was that he had moved faster than the others, that he had reached the opposite edge of the woods before anyone else around him. But within a few minutes, others began to catch up. They hunkered down at the edge of the trees and looked down the valley toward a little group of houses—what the lieutenant had called a village. Ted soon came over. "There are two *Panzer*s behind that barn down there," he said.

"I know. You can see the back end of them."

"There must be Krauts in those houses."

That was obvious, and yet it was a strange thought. Just a few hundred meters away, men were getting up, or having breakfast—like men getting up to go to work. There was smoke coming from the chimneys, and the houses looked nice, like a picture on a postcard, with snow-covered roofs and icicles hanging from the eaves. It looked like a little place that ought to be peaceful, ought to be left that way.

Lieutenant Nowland was moving through the trees, talking to the men. "Stay back. Don't get yourselves spotted," he told them. And then he whispered, "We're going to go straight at them, get across this open area just as quickly as we can, and take them by surprise. That means you have to get to those houses before they get their tanks going. Once you start down this hill, don't stop. If they throw some mortars at us, or get some small-arms fire going, you'll think you're safer to drop down into the snow. But if you do that, it's just a matter of time until they get you. The only way to break them loose from those houses is to get down the hill quick and get some grenades inside." He moved the men into another skirmish line and spread them out across the top ridge, inside the trees. "Don't bunch up," he kept telling everyone. "Don't give them any easy targets. When I say, 'Move out,' we all go at once."

Spence wasn't cold now. He had forgotten about the pain in his feet, about the discomfort of the night before. Ted whispered, "Maybe we can sleep in those houses tonight," but Spence couldn't even think of that. What he knew was that he was going to be running straight at the enemy, right to their doorstep. It was something like that first jump out of an airplane. He knew that very soon he would do what he had to do, but only if he didn't think. His instincts were saying, "Duck down. Don't go."

When the command came, Spence ran harder than most. He was in great shape and had strong legs, even if they weren't very long. He wanted off that open slope as fast as he could make it, and so he loped, pulling his knees high—like elk he had watched back home. And nothing happened. Everything was still out in the morning air—except for the grunts and gasps of the men, the rattle of their equipment on their belts. They were more than halfway down the hill, no longer in much of a line, when Spence heard the first *ping*. It was nothing, like the pop of a breaking light globe, and one simple *buzz*, like the ones he remembered from his deer hunting days. But a man to his right went down—hit by the bullet or scared to be hit. Then there was a second *ping*, a second *buzz*, and this time the thud of the bullet in the snow, very close. Spence's knee buckled, and he almost dove down, but he wanted off this field of white, this target area. He drove himself forward.

By then a chugging sound had begun—like a motorcycle engine. And off to Spence's left the air was all full of thumping sounds. Machine-gun fire, Spence realized, and at the same time he knew the mistake he had made: He was out front, a good target. He had come maybe three hundred meters and had about two hundred still to go. But he didn't slow down. He had to get all that open space out of the way, had to get in next to those houses.

The bullets were whizzing, tracers flying, and ahead of him was a stone fence that cut across the hill. He kept working hard, hopping, pulling against the snow that clung to his feet, but when the buzzes turned into whistles and filled the air right around him, he took a few more steps and then dove down behind the fence. And it felt good to get down. Bullets pounded into the snow, cracked off the stones of the low fence, but he was behind it, safe. Other men were diving down alongside him, but Spence heard the lieutenant scream, "You can't stop. You're dead men if you do."

And in that instant Spence saw the truth in what the lieutenant was saying. He heard a thump, down by the houses, and a second later, felt an explosion nearby, saw dirt and ice fly. The Germans were getting their mortars going now, and one had hit not twenty feet away. When he felt the crash of debris against his steel helmet, he thought for a moment that he was filled with shrapnel, but no pain struck him—he was all right. Now he had to go again. As he jumped up, the whistling was all around him, and he felt something grab at his coat, rip at his forearm like barbed wire. But he ran, anyway.

He stumbled and rolled, turned over in the snow, and knew even then that his awkward lurch had saved his life, but he scrambled up and ran a few more steps, rolled again, and kept tumbling forward. And somewhere in the confusion, he caught sight of the muzzle fire of a machine gun in the second-floor window of the first house. He knew that was the enemy, the danger that had to be dealt with.

He came up scrambling again, and this time felt something rip at his foot, send it flying out from under him. He cartwheeled again, but rolled back up to his feet before he was ever really down. He was now just fifty meters away, and he turned the final run into a burst. He wanted to sprint, but the snow was still clinging to his feet, like he was running in a bad dream. When he hit a spot where the snow was not so deep, he made a final charge to the wall outside the first house. When he dropped down behind it, he knew he couldn't stay. He was closer to that machine gun than anyone. He had the best chance of taking it out. He pulled a grenade loose from his belt and then slung his M-1 rifle over his shoulder. He leaped onto the rock wall, rolled over it, and broke to the door of the house. He ran hard, pulled the pin on the grenade, and rolled it ahead of him toward the door. Then he slammed himself against the wall of the house and ducked his head.

The grenade went off, showering him with debris, but as soon as he could look up, he could see that the door was gone. Someone was with him by then. Spence swung the rifle off his shoulder, and when the other soldier—a guy from his platoon named Erickson—broke inside the house, he followed. They ended up side by side, pivoting their rifles, ready for any movement. But the gun was upstairs, and the popping sound hadn't stopped. Erickson broke up the stairs, and Spence followed again. But as Erickson hit the top of the stairs, he seemed to explode. Blood splattered in all directions, and Erickson's body was thrown back down the stairs on top of Spence. Both men fell backward, crashed to the floor at the foot of the steps, but Spence pushed Erickson off himself and came up quickly. He jerked another grenade from his belt, ran halfway up the stairs, slammed himself against the wall, pulled the pin, then threw the grenade up the stairs and through the open door just as a German soldier stepped out. The grenade rolled past the man's legs, and then blew up behind him. The explosion blasted from the room, and the German was thrown face first onto the stairs. He hit and stayed, and Spence merely watched, too shocked to think of going back downstairs for his rifle. But when the soldier didn't move, Spence waited a second or two, then fumbled at his belt, found another grenade, pulled the pin, jumped up the stairs a few more steps, and rolled it into the room. He waited, pinned himself once more, and heard the detonation. Then he hurried down the stairs, saw Erickson, now lying in a pool of blood, his legs torn mostly off, his mouth hanging wide open.

But Spence did what he had been trained to do. He grabbed his rifle, pulled it out from under Erickson, and then he charged back to the upstairs room. He came in spraying bullets at nothing, at anything. He shattered a mirror, shot through a chest of drawers, and thumped a couple of bullets into a German who was on the floor next to his machine gun. But the man's face was smashed into the hardwood floor, sideways, and blood was running from his nose, his mouth, his eyes.

Spence stared at the man. And then at another soldier next to him: a young kid who had apparently been feeding bullets to the gunner. The boy didn't seem hurt. There was no blood, no sign of damage. He was lying on his back by a baby cradle, and he seemed to be resting, almost as though he had been spilled from that cradle without waking up. He was clearly younger than Spence. He might have been fifteen, but he looked twelve—he reminded Spence of Lloyd. He was little, with delicate hands, stained from the metal ammunition belts he had been handling. His eyes were open halfway, dark blue.

Now boots were thudding up the stairs, and Spence spun around. But these were guys from his platoon. "Nice work," someone said. The lieutenant. "You're going to get a medal for this, Private Morgan."

Spence stared at him. He couldn't think what the words could mean. Couldn't Nowland see this little boy on the floor? Hadn't he seen Erickson downstairs?

"Are you hit? Looks like your arm is bleeding." Spence looked down, saw the tear in his coat, the blood. He had forgotten about that.

CHAPTER 12

It was the first day of 1945. For two days Dieter's company had stayed put. Once their forward movement had bogged down, they had dug in and held on. Now they were being hit, off and on, by artillery fire, so the men couldn't stray very far from their foxholes. To Dieter it was maddening, all this sitting. On the days when the sky was clear, American fighters had become a constant menace, and yet, Dieter had seen almost no German air power.

As night fell, Dieter and Schaefer huddled low in their foxhole to keep as warm as possible, but they said nothing. And Dieter hated the silence as much as anything, these nights that seemed to come in the middle of the afternoon and last almost until the next night. How could a man fight, show himself for the hero he was, when he spent his life huddled in a hole, just trying not to freeze? He pulled a blanket over his head and pressed his face against his arm. His cheeks were stinging. But when he shut his eyes this way, the same images always came to mind: his home, the light inside, the warmth from his fireplace. Food had been scarce for many Germans for the last couple of years, but the Hedricks had eaten well on the farm. They had always had fresh potatoes, chickens to kill, and they had drunk plenty of fresh milk. He longed for that now, some warm milk and some of his mother's homemade bread. Or the cherry *Kuchen* his mother baked on summer mornings before the kitchen heated up. He remembered the smell of it when he walked into the house after doing his morning chores, or after returning from the creek, where he and his friends liked to swim on summer days. He tried to think of other things, but he kept wishing he could go back to that time—back to his glorious days in the Hitler Youth when the younger boys looked up to him and no one ever talked like Schaefer. Dieter's rise in the *HJ* had been the great achievement of his life. He had started out as such a little boy in *Jungvolk*, small for his age, and timid, but each time he had met the test, had proved himself, he had risen in the esteem of the other boys. Finally he had gotten his growth, was as tall and strong as anyone, and by then he was a confident defender of the principles that good German boys believed. He could give commands, teach the younger boys. And he had seen in their eyes how much they had wanted to be like him, just as he had once wanted to be like Hans Keller.

The problem was, he was surrounded by lesser men now, and he was stuck with Schaefer, of all people, who must surely have foreign blood running in his veins, who was not half a German, not a tenth of what a great German soldier should be. Dieter had to concentrate on his medal, on the way he had felt that day the *Führer* had looked him in the eye and asked him for a commitment never to stop fighting. And that's what he would do, too. He would keep his promise. He wouldn't think so much about cherry *Kuchen*, about Mother and his warm house. He wouldn't fuss about the cold. He would be ready when the call came to thrust the Americans out of Bastogne. He would do his part and much more. He would show these dolts around him what heroism was all about.

So it was a great relief when Sergeant Franke came to him and Schaefer that night and said, "We're going to start a push in the morning, and our company will take the lead this time. We'll clear these woods in front of us, and then our whole battalion will make a thrust toward the south. We need to break through the enemy lines and take Bastogne. It's crucial to our entire operation, and we've let the Americans hold out too long."

This was the kind of talk Dieter had been waiting for. When Franke left, Dieter even took a chance and said, "Schaefer, this is it. Tomorrow we can fight like lions. We can prove ourselves. Wouldn't you like to sleep in a nice, warm house in Bastogne tomorrow night?"

Schaefer hesitated for a time, and then, in a quiet voice, said, "Dieter, stay alongside me. The important thing is that tomorrow night, you're still alive."

Dieter rejected the words, casting them aside with a laugh and a wave of his hand. But he did think of dying, of lying dead in the snow. He had seen the bodies, frozen, gray, eyes staring. He told himself that once he was dead, it wouldn't matter what became of his body, but what he feared was nothingness—that if he died, there would be nothing at all. He knew that a hero shouldn't fear death, but where was the glory in dying for his country and never knowing it—just lying on the battlefield, gray and hard as ice? It was nice to think of a statue in his village, at least a placard with his name on it, but it wouldn't happen, he supposed, and even if it did, what would it mean to him, once he was one of those frozen corpses?

It was a long night. He slept at times, but never long enough to push much night behind him, and the black— which only forced the idea of death into his head—clung like nausea. It stretched time, made it seem worse even than the cold. His winter uniform, his white coveralls, his gloves, his woolen hat—it all helped, but cold had gotten down inside him, and his body felt as though it would never be warm again.

Before daylight Dieter was up with the other men in his company. He ate from his bread sack—black bread and canned meat—and then he set out in the dark, struggling through the snow. The movement was good. He liked the return of blood to his feet and hands. He marched through the trees and then heard the whispered command: "We wait now. The other companies are moving up to join us. When first light breaks, we start our move, and we don't let anything stop us."

This was it. Dieter finally had his chance. He waited while his breath continued to pump, the steam flooding over his face, his heart pulsing in his ears. Long after he was cooling down, getting his breath, his heart continued its drumbeat. And he told himself that was good. He was ready and alive, not hiding in a dark hole any longer.

As light broke, the men moved forward, worked their way, in a line, through the trees. What Dieter hadn't expected was to feel so separated from the others. Schaefer stayed with him, to his right, and off to his left he caught glimpses of Franke at times, but they were moving through trees that were covered with snow, trees all the same size, and the snow sucked up most of the sound. It was as though Dieter were marching into battle alone, with only Schaefer alongside him. He wished that he had marched with Sergeant Franke, or someone else who wanted this victory as much as he did.

But there was no victory, exactly—just hard walking, with his boots breaking through the crusted snow and sinking to his ankles on some steps, all the way to his knee on others. The snow had drifted through the trees unevenly. When he would sink to his knee, he would have to straggle to free his foot, and then, on the next step, sink again. It was easy to forget about the enemy, to worry only about moving ahead.

And then Dieter heard the sound he had learned to hate: the high whine that deepened and then ended in a sucking gust just before the concussion. "Get down," Schaefer shouted, but Dieter didn't have to make that decision. His knees had already given way. He was flat on his face in the snow, and when the explosion broke in the trees just ahead, he heard the crash of limbs, the whir of metal in the air. Back in his foxhole, he had told himself that the shell would have to hit right into his hole to get him, and if that happened, he would never know it. But out here, those slashing chunks of metal could cut through his body and leave a string of intestines across the snow. They could spatter his skull, his brain, in all directions, or even worse, they could rip off a leg or an arm, and leave a man screaming, berserk, desperate for help. He had seen all that already, and however brave he wanted to be, he was frozen to the ground now, terrified that the next shell would strike closer.

For the better part of an hour the noise continued. The explosions were often far off, and Dieter would breathe during that time, wondering whether any soldiers in his company were being hit, but then the guns would shift their aim, and for a time, the shells would come in his direction again. They would shatter the trees, seem to crack the air into pieces, and send a shock of concussion over him, sucking him upward, and then the whistling shrapnel would shoot over him, around him, crashing off trees, knocking limbs down. And sometimes, a scream would follow. "Medic! Help me! Help me." The sound was always so wild and desperate, as though the man were being burned with scalding water.

When the bombardment finally ended, Sergeant Franke gave the quiet a little time, and then he shouted through the woods, "All right. Now we move again. We're all right. We don't have ground troops in front of us."

But Schaefer whispered to Dieter, "Be careful. The *Amis* like to pause and give us time to get up, and then they hit us again."

But it didn't happen. Schaefer had thought of the worst again, and he had been wrong. All morning the men trudged through the woods, and they confronted no one. Dieter saw no sign, in fact, that enemy troops had ever been here. That only proved how wrong Schaefer was—how wrong all the cowards had been, all those who had held up for several days instead of marching into Bastogne. Dieter had a feeling that his unit could leave these trees, catch a good road, and thrust straight into town.

Early in the afternoon the men came to a little road

that cut through the woods, and Captain Schmidt had them stop. It was a chance to reform the skirmish line, to get everyone moving along together again. It was also a chance to eat. Dieter was happy for the rest, but he hoped this delay wouldn't last long. His company had to move fast to accomplish something today—something more than "clearing" a woods that was empty already. What he feared most was that they would stop soon and start digging in again. Once the digging started, all there was to wait for was another night.

Dieter was sitting by the edge of the road, a piece of bread in one hand and a chunk of old cheese in the other. He had taken both his gloves off, but he wasn't cold. The clouds had broken up a little, and the sun was actually shining.

But then he heard a buzzing sound. It wasn't artillery, wasn't a truck. He started, looked around, but didn't know what he was hearing until Schaefer screamed, "Fighters!" The airplanes were there, instantly. Two of them. They came in low over the trees, and by the time Dieter moved, they were already strafing straight down the road. *Whap! Whap! Whap!*

Dieter had heard all three thumps in the snow, not more than a meter or two in front of him. If he had moved faster, he would have stepped right into them. It was his indecision that had saved his life. But now he was moving. He jumped and tripped, fell, but scrambled up and stumbled into the woods. He kept running even after he was under cover of the trees. He found a place where brush had grown up around the base of a fir tree, and he dove inside.

He had no idea where Schaefer was, and he felt the loss immediately. The fighters came back, swept along the edge of the woods, and this time fired blindly into the trees. The men were scattered, and the trees stopped most of the bullets this time, but as soon as the fighters passed over and were gone, Dieter heard Schaefer. "Hedrick, where are you?"

"Over here."

Dieter didn't move, stayed in the cover, but he looked out enough to see Schaefer coming his way. "They won't come back," he said. "Not unless they have ammunition to waste. We never should have let ourselves get caught in the open like that."

Dieter hadn't thought of airplanes, but with the clearing skies, he should have.

By then, Franke was walking over. "The lieutenant says to dig in here," he said. "Under these trees. We'll make another thrust in the morning."

Dieter didn't admit it to himself, but he felt some relief at the idea, no matter what he had thought earlier. He got out his entrenching tool, and he and Schaefer dug their hole very close to the tree, partly under it. The ground was not as hard here where the needles had fallen and insulated the ground under the snow, and he and Schaefer made fast progress. After a time, however, Schaefer took a rest to breathe, and when he did, he asked Dieter, "Where are your gloves?"

Dieter hadn't needed them yet, but he had thought of them. They were back by the road. He knew he would go back for them, but he hadn't been in any hurry to walk out into the open. "I'll go get them," he said. "I left them where we were eating."

"I'll get them," Schaefer said.

"No, I can."

"You dig. I'm tired of digging. I'll get your gloves."

That was fine with Dieter, but he wished Schaefer would stop telling him what to do. Maybe the man was a corporal, but he didn't really take his rank seriously. He didn't talk to Dieter as a military leader—but like a grown-up dealing with a child.

Schaefer was gone much too long, and when he finally returned, he said, "They're gone. You shouldn't have left them out there so long."

"What do you mean, gone?"

"Just what I said. Someone with old gloves, full of holes, was just happy to have them."

"One of our own men—from our company?"

"Sure."

"No one would do that. German soldiers don't steal from one another."

"It's not your fault you're a fool, Dieter, but at least start to learn from your mistakes."

"What do you mean? Soldiers steal from their comrades? Is that what you want me to learn? I don't believe it. You looked in the wrong place. I'll go look myself."

"No. It's pointless. Men have to survive. If you don't return for your gloves, someone has to assume you're a dead man. That's the way it is out here."

"What can I do? Where can I get gloves?"

"You can't. I'll give you mine. I know how to manage."

"No. Absolutely not."

Schaefer had begun to dig, but now he raised his head, slowly, and he said, "Fine. Have it your way."

By the time the hole was dug, the sun was low in the west, and with the clearer skies, the cold was coming on fast. Dieter got into his hole, ate again, and then tucked his hands inside his coat pockets. But that wasn't enough. His hands had gotten too cold, and his pockets couldn't produce the heat he needed to get his circulation back. He could feel already that if he didn't do something soon, he would never make it through the night without frostbite. He unbuttoned his coat, trying to be quiet about it. What he didn't want was for Schaefer to know that he was struggling. He crossed his arms and worked his hands inside his coat along his sides, and for a time that didn't seem too bad. But the cold gradually intensified, and Dieter was feeling it, especially now, with his coat gaping open at the neck. He could also feel his frustration building.

"Put your hands in here," Schaefer said.

"What?"

"In my coat. I'm bigger than you. I make more heat."

"I'm all right. I'm doing fine."

"Will you be doing fine when they cut your fingers off? You won't be able to pull any triggers then—or milk your old cow, when they send you home."

Still, Dieter didn't move.

"Lean forward. Give me your hands."

Dieter pulled his hands from his coat and reached forward, but he was humiliated.

"Button your coat."

Dieter fumbled with the buttons, and the effort sent shooting pains through his fingers, but he got his coat tightened around his neck, and then he reached forward again. He didn't say a word, but he heard Schaefer pull up the sweater inside his coat and then felt him grip Dieter's wrists. He pulled one of Dieter's hands and then the other deep under his arms, against his warm body, and then he clamped his arms down over them.

Dieter liked the warmth, but not the dependence or the cost this was to Schaefer. "Your coat is wide open," Dieter finally said.

"I'm all right." Dieter knew what he had to do, but the

idea was repulsive, angering. "I'll lean against you so you won't freeze."

It was the logical thing to do. The man's coat was open, and Dieter could press his chest against Schaefer's, keep the front of him warm while Dieter's hands were warming. It was almost more than Dieter could stand, but he leaned forward, laid his head against Schaefer's shoulder, and pressed his chest against the man's front. He rested there for a moment, liking the warmth and comfort more than he ever could have suspected, but was shocked when he realized that—for no reason he understood—he felt as though he was about to cry.

But he didn't cry. What he did was go to sleep, resting against Schaefer's chest, feeling almost warm, almost safe.

CHAPTER 13

"Okay, men, listen up." Lieutenant Nowland was striding toward the men of the platoon, many of whom were gathered around little fires. They were heating coffee, thawing out K-ration cans. Spence didn't like the serious look on the lieutenant's face.

Nowland asked the men to gather around him, and then he said, "We've spotted a company of Krauts in that forest down off this hill. We're going after them."

"Across an open field?" Sergeant Pappas asked.

"Yes." Pappas cursed quietly, but he didn't have to say what he thought. Everyone knew. Men were going to die today.

"Sergeant, that's enough. In case you haven't learned the concept yet, in a war we engage the enemy. We can't do that from here."

Pappas took a long breath. He knew ten times more

about fighting a war than Nowland did. "I understand that, sir," he finally said. "But do they have tanks?"

That was almost always the problem for Airborne divisions. The Germans they were facing were mostly armored units, but paratroopers weren't equipped with tanks.

"The captain didn't say anything about tanks," Nowland said. "He just said we're all going in—the whole company. Finish up what you're doing. At 0800 we jump off."

Spence didn't want to eat anything more. He tossed a half-eaten can of SPAM into the snow. It made a hole the shape of the can, and all Spence could think about was putting his foot into that snow, hiking all the way down the hill, straight into enemy fire.

Last time he had done that, he had made it—by luck, as much as anything—but it was hard to believe he could get that lucky again. He had taken a hit in the arm that day, but the bullet had only bit a hunk of flesh out of his forearm, just below his elbow, and the medics had dressed it, there in the field, and hadn't even sent him back to an aid station. Another bullet had torn a chunk from the heel of his boot. At times now, Spence wished that one of those bullets had done enough damage to get him sent to a hospital, at least until spring. He was scared of being killed, and tired of the cold, but there was more to it than that. He hadn't been able to stop thinking about the young boy he had killed, or Erickson, who had been torn in half only because he had gone up the stairs first, ahead of Spence. When he tried to go to sleep at night, he kept seeing all that, like movies, playing back.

At 0800, the order came: "Move out. Stay spread out. Five yards between you and the next guy." Spence looked over at Ted. The skin around Ted's eyes was drained of blood; his lips were white. Up and down the line, no one was talking. Spence was having trouble getting his breath, but he stepped into the opening. It was 600 yards down this hill—something like that—but he was relieved when he had gone twenty and no one had fired on him. He told himself it was just a hard walk, in deep snow, but that no one was watching him from the woods at the bottom of the hill—not like last time.

It was hard going, the same hard going he had known so often lately. Every step was a fight as he tugged his boot back out of the hard-crusted snow. In only a few minutes he was breathing deep, feeling his lungs start to labor, and in another couple of minutes he felt himself begin to sweat inside his heavy overcoat and uniform. He was carrying a musette bag over his shoulder, with extra socks and underwear, and at his waist, attached to his webbing gear, were a canteen, knife, first aid kit, compass, grenades, and his entrenching tool. Besides that, his pockets were full of K-ration cans. All of it was heavy and only made things harder.

But halfway down the hill there was still no fire, no sign of the enemy. He began to think about the hole he would dig that night, probably in these woods. He hoped the dirt was softer there. And then a thought occurred to him, and he felt a load lift from his shoulders. Those Germans had been dug in. If they had cleared out, they had left some nice foxholes behind. He could spend his time fixing a hole up, enlarging it, covering it, and maybe he would get a nice night's rest, for once.

It was a good thought, and he was still moving ahead, no problem. After 400 yards or so, the ground leveled out, which actually made the walking a little harder. He was getting a little ahead of the others, and so he held up for a moment to catch his breath. He was looking around, actually thinking how pretty the snow was on the trees, when he heard someone gasp, "Tanks!"

Spence scanned the woods to the end. Off to the left, crawling around the trees, were two big German tanks. Tigers. Their long guns—88s—were swinging around toward him. At the same moment, Spence's eyes were pulled back to the woods, where something had moved. He saw three men, in white suits, run into the opening. One was carrying something over his head; he looked as though he had a thin, black horn growing out of his forehead. He dropped down, and the other two men dropped to their knees with him. They were setting up a machine gun, a big MG42. Off to the right of the threesome, another team was doing the same thing. And now soldiers with rifles were emerging from the trees.

Spence had already spun around by the time he heard the command, "Fall back! Fall back!"

This was a trap. There was nowhere to go but back up the hill, no reasonable cover to the left or right. The woods back at the top of this long incline seemed miles away, but that's what he had to get to. Spence had no time to think, only to run, but he already knew what was about to happen, and somewhere in his consciousness was an obvious truth. Some officer, somewhere, had made an absolutely stupid decision to send him into such a mess.

For about ten steps, Spence tried to run all out. But he knew immediately that his body wouldn't hold out. He couldn't last a hundred yards running that hard, and he had 400 to go, maybe more. And so he slowed to a reasonable pace, slogged hard, jerked his feet from the snow, reached as long as he could, stepped again, and made what wobbling progress he could. And every second, he expected a bullet in his back. The machine guns had already begun to chatter.

The first of the 88s' shells hit to Spence's right. He heard the familiar *whomp* as it thumped into the snow, and he saw the dark earth spatter over the white, up the hill ahead of him. He heard men screaming, too. What he didn't do was look around. He concentrated on the snow in front of him, trying to step where he—or someone else—had stepped before, on the way down. But it didn't help, and when two more shells struck, almost at the same time, the concussion knocked him off his feet. One shell had hit close, and he had seen a steel helmet fly past him, had heard the grunt of a man who must have died too quickly to feel the pain.

But he still didn't look, didn't glance back. He fought his way back onto his feet and kept driving himself up the hill. The buzz of machine-gun fire was around him, the bullets pounding into the snow. He was moving as fast as anyone, faster than most, but he didn't think about that, didn't think much of anything except that there was no chance to make it to the top. He was breathing too hard already. He remembered that old agony, the searing sickness in his lungs that he had known during those agonizing training runs back in Georgia, and he knew his limits. He could go another fifty yards, perhaps, but his legs would never take him to the top. He tried to step too long, stumbled, and went down on his face, and he felt bullets whap around him. For a moment be thought of staying down, playing dead, but another spray of bullets brought him back to his feet. As he came up he threw off his musette bag and then tore off his heavy coat. For a few steps he felt lighter, and he burst ahead. He tried to imagine that he was a harder target, farther from the bullets and the big shells, smaller without that coat. But then the guy next to him went down. He cursed, and Spence heard the gurgle in his voice, knew that he would die. Spence didn't hesitate, didn't think of stopping to help his comrade, didn't even wonder whether it might be Ted.

Shells were crashing into the earth, spraying mud, mostly to the distant side of the hill now, away from Spence. But the machine guns kept pounding, and a guy almost in front of Spence went down. How had that happened? How had a bullet gotten through him—over him or past him—and hit a man in the same path?

The man was screaming at God, swearing, but also praying. As Spence trudged past, the soldier rolled onto his back, and Spence saw a bloody glob, the guy's insides hanging out of him.

Spence kept going, but he fell again, face first, into the snow. As he came up, his hand rumbled for his webbing, and he released the other things he was carrying—his ammunition, canteen, everything. And that helped. He willed himself back onto his feet and kept hold of his rifle. It crossed his mind, vaguely, that he was running from battle, that he should actually turn and fire his weapon. But he knew he couldn't do that. Maybe he knew it was useless; maybe he was following the command to fall back; maybe he was only doing what everyone else was doing. But the fear inside him was screaming, "Don't look back. They'll see you. They'll shoot you."

He was driving his left foot forward, rather off

balance, when something hit him in the head. It banged off his helmet, sending him flying. He plunged into the snow, confused. He had taken a hit, he was sure, but he felt no pain, only the burning in his lungs. His legs were leaden now, too dead to go on. He stayed in the snow and decided to take his chances on the ground. Maybe he was hurt; maybe medics would come for him and fix him up, take him to a hospital.

But Sergeant Pappas's voice was suddenly there, screaming at him, and he felt someone grasp his arm. "Get up, Morgan. Keep going. They'll kill you if you stay down."

Maybe the few breaths, the seconds of rest, had helped, because he expected to fall down again when he tried to get up, but he got his legs under him and drove forward again. And he realized he was closer to the top than he had thought. He finally looked to the woods above, not just at the snow in front of him. He saw he had only a hundred yards or so to go—like that last kick in a race—and he was out in front of almost everyone. He didn't know how many had fallen, didn't know how many were behind him, but there was comfort in being the most distant target, comfort in the thought that in those trees was dark cover, a place to hide.

And then a new thunder opened up. A series of tremendous thuds shook him, almost knocked him over. What terrorized him was the realization that the sound was in front. Were the Germans shooting from both sides now? Was there nowhere to go?

He came to a stop, in spite of himself, and it took a moment to accept what he suddenly realized: The guns were his—American. Big 105s. And they were firing down the hill *at* the Germans.

The sound was like trains flying overhead, like the sky breaking apart, but the guns had saved him, and Spence knew it. He pushed ahead again. He lumbered on through the snow, and finally he glanced back. The tanks were turning, dropping back. The machine-gun teams had already disappeared. Spence sank to his knees, bent forward, tried to get his breath. But he wouldn't really feel safe until he was off this hill. He breathed for a time, then forced himself up one more time and, wobbling, put one foot ahead of the other. He glanced around and saw that others were catching up, also finishing their retreat. Something like half the men had made it—many more than seemed possible. Most had dropped their gear, the same as he had. He was relieved not to be the only one.

He staggered into the trees and dropped on his back, but he was sick. He rolled onto his side and expected to vomit. Lieutenant Nowland stopped next to him. "Good job," he said. "Good job, Morgan. That was some run."

"I tossed my gear," Spence said, wanting to confess, wanting to find a reason to be angry with himself.

"We all did. At least you have your rifle. Some of the guys dumped their weapons, too."

Spence was glad to know that. He didn't want to believe that he was a coward. But as he lay there gasping, he finally got a chance to think, and he realized what he needed to know. "Did Ted make it?"

"Who?"

"Draney?"

"I don't know. I haven't seen him. Do what you've got to do here for a minute, but when you can walk, head over to where we were this morning. We'll go back to the same holes."

"All right." But now Spence was frightened. He got to his knees, breathed some more, and then stood up and looked around. A guy named Slocum, a fellow from his squad, was lying in the snow not far away, still heaving for breath.

"Did you see Draney?"

Slocum couldn't talk yet. He drew in air for a long time before he said, "Draney went down. I saw him on the ground, on his back."

Spence took a step toward the hill. "Where?"

"I don't know. Way down there."

"Where?" Spence was going back down the hill. He had to.

"He's dead, Morgan. His chest was bleeding. He wasn't yelling or nothing. He was gone."

That wasn't good enough. Spence had to find him. Medics might be able to fix him up. He walked to the clearing at the top of the hill, where the last of the men were down on the ground, still trying to breathe. He went on past, starting down the hill.

"Morgan, where are you going?" Sergeant Pappas yelled at him.

"Draney," was all Spence could manage to say.

"Let the medics do what they can down there—when they can. You can't walk down and back again."

Spence was angry, and it was mostly because Pappas was right. He couldn't make it down and back. And Slocum was probably right. Ted really was dead. Spence knelt in the snow again, and finally he vomited. But that only relieved him of the sickness in his gut. And suddenly he was furious. He hadn't known it would be like this, hadn't understood what he was getting into when he had signed up. Some idiot had sent the company down that hill, sacrificed them for no good reason. Who was running this war? Did they know what they were doing? Did anyone even care that Ted had died for nothing?

Spence wanted to be angry, stay angry. He wanted to hate someone for this. But the anger was hard to hold. Out there in the snow, without a coat, he began to cool, began to weaken, feel the pain in his arm—feel everything. But he didn't want to walk back to the men, didn't want to hear what Nowland or any of the rest of them had to say.

It was Pappas who finally walked out to Spence. "Look, Morgan," he said, "I know that's real tough—losing your buddy. But we gotta get you over to a fire or you'll get so cold inside, you'll never survive the night. We've got some guys going down to bring back the coats and gear and everything, but you won't get that stuff for a while."

Spence got to his feet, and then he turned and looked at Pappas.

"I lost my partner, too," Pappas said. "Barela is down there on the hill with Draney. You and me, we might as well dig in together." He put his hand on Spence's shoulder. "You'll be all right. The best thing is, don't think about it too much. Just keep doing what you gotta do. That's the one thing I've learned. You can't let all this stuff get in your head too much."

Spence didn't agree with that, not at all. He couldn't just forget Ted. The idea was almost sickening. And yet the kindness in the sarge's voice reached him, meant something. He turned back around, looked down the hill. He had started to cry, and he didn't want Pappas to see that. He tried to control himself, not let go, but sobs were breaking from him, shaking him, and he felt like a stupid little boy.

"That's okay, Morgan," Sergeant Pappas said. "Give it a minute, and then come on over."

And that's all that Spence could do. But if he could have, he would have traded places with Ted, let him have his chance to get home to see his family.

CHAPTER 14

When the first crash of artillery struck, Dieter heard the sound behind him, the shell bursting in the trees. "Fall back," he heard his sergeant shout, but his instinct was not to do that, not to run into the very trees where the shell had just hit. Besides, there were still Americans on the hill, maybe half of them still alive and moving. Dieter wanted to keep shooting.

But the next crash was much closer, and Dieter heard a scream, saw mud spatter. And again he heard his sergeant. "Drop back into the woods and keep going."

This time Dieter didn't hesitate. He ran hard, fought through the snow, reached the trees, and kept moving. He knew where the hole was that he and Schaefer had slept in the night before—or thought he did—and wanted to get to it. But the trees were confusing, the trails trampled, and he wasn't sure where he was going. He ran, kept plunging downward through the wooded area, and now the artillery shells were striking in the trees. A few minutes before, he had felt the thrill of seeing the *Amis* on the run, trying so hard to fight their way up that long hill. Now all that was forgotten. He heard the shrapnel spinning through the trees, and he expected any second to be hit.

And then someone grabbed his arm, and he twisted to see Schaefer. "This way," he shouted, and he broke to his left. Schaefer was right, too. He ran ahead, not very fast, but directly to the hole he and Dieter had dug. He stopped and let Dieter drop in, and then he climbed in with him. They ducked down, and Dieter felt much safer.

Schaefer was breathing hard, his face splotchy from the effort. "I'm too old for this," he muttered.

Dieter laughed. He felt the exhilaration now. He and Schaefer were all right. Dieter had learned to accept the sound of artillery shells, not to feel the panic he had in those first days. And now he was remembering what he had done. He had shot some of those Americans. He was certain that he had put down at least a couple of them himself. "They won't get many of us," he said, "and we cut their numbers in half. Tomorrow, we'll attack again, and we'll drive them back. I guess we're doing all right for ourselves."

"Yes. For now."

"What's wrong with you, Schaefer? You never take

any joy—not even in our victories." Dieter didn't want to be angry with the man. Schaefer had gotten Dieter through the night. He had warmed his hands, inside his coat, and then, once Dieter was doing better, had given him his own gloves. Schaefer had survived the night with his hands tucked inside his coat, and now he was using a double pair of socks for mittens. When Dieter had begged him to take his own gloves back, Schaefer had absolutely refused. In some ways, all that bothered Dieter; he didn't want to be treated as a child. But still, the man, however gruff—however misguided—could be kind, and Dieter did appreciate that.

"On the eastern front we would throw back the Russians sometimes, and always, the next day, they would come back all the more determined—and with reinforcements. There was never any end to them. They just kept coming."

"It isn't that way here."

"Maybe. I don't know. Those are big guns they're firing at us. If they stay after us, they can do some heavy damage."

Dieter leaned back and breathed. He could still hear artillery, but it wasn't zeroed in on this part of the woods. The bursts rumbled through the trees—no more frightening than a distant storm. Dieter was proud of himself that he was learning how things were, that he wasn't frightened by every little noise any longer. "We took care of them today, in any case. Did you see how many of them went down?"

"Yes. I saw."

Dieter was still excited. He squirmed a little in the hole and found more room for his legs. "Did you get a few yourself? I did."

"I don't know."

"You must be a good shot by now, Schaefer. You probably killed more than I did."

Schaefer didn't respond. Dieter could see his face, shadowed, his growing whiskers, his tired eyes, but he couldn't see any emotion. He didn't know what the man was thinking, but the silence seemed a censure, and it was maddening. "Don't tell me you're not happy for every *Ami*, and for every Russian, you can put away? If you say that, I'll know you're a traitor."

Again, Schaefer said nothing. "Well, which is it? Are you proud for the enemy you've killed or not?"

Schaefer took a breath, still rough from the running, and then he said, "Dieter, be quiet. Let's get some rest. I'm tired."

"I want to know whether you're on our side or not. I need to know what kind of a man I'm stuck with."

Schaefer's hands came up, those dark stockings, palms out. "Enough," they seemed to say. "Stop."

"I tell myself, these are the men who will rape my sisters, who will kill my parents and take away my farm.

These are the men who want to destroy my country. I have no problem taking their lives before they take ours. Maybe you're soft inside, Schaefer; maybe you shed tears for these men who fall in front of us, but I'm not like you. I know what I'm fighting for."

"Dieter, I'll tell you what you're fighting for." But this was something new. Dieter heard a kind of rage in Schaefer, not in the volume of his voice, but in the tightness. "I'll tell you what I saw in Poland. I was in Warsaw, after I was shot. I was in the hospital there for over a month. I met a man who knew what was happening. He didn't try to hide it—he bragged about it."

"What? What do you mean?"

"Most of the Jews who have been gathered up in Germany, across Europe, that's where they've been taken, to Poland. They live in ghettos, in filthy, stinking apartments, with barely enough food to survive."

"It's what they've brought upon themselves, Schaefer. You know what the *Führer* says. We must do hard things to set the world right."

"Listen to me, Dieter. I want you to know this." He was breathing harder now, as though he had been running again.

Dieter was frightened. He had some idea what was coming, and he didn't want to hear it. "Don't start with the lies that the Jews themselves spread. I won't listen to that kind of nonsense."

"Dieter, do you know any Jews?"

"What do you mean?"

"Have you ever known a Jew? Even one?"

"I had a friend, in school, when I was young. A boy named Aaron. But that was before I learned all about them, the way they are."

"What did you learn? Was Aaron filthy, Dieter? Did he do anything to harm anyone? Was he dangerous?"

"He was just a boy."

"What about his parents, then? What problems did they cause?"

"I don't know."

"Then answer me this: Where are they now?"

"I have no idea," Dieter said.

"Are they living near your home somewhere, where they did before?"

"No."

"Where did they go?"

"I told you. I don't know." But Dieter did know something. Aaron's family had been forced to leave, forced to board a train and take nothing more than suitcases with them. When Dieter had asked about it, his father had merely said, "It's not our business, son. It's better not to ask about these things." But after, in the Hitler Youth, when Dieter had heard the disturbing, nasty truth about Jews, how they controlled the money supply, and hated Christians, caused terrible problems with their deceit and lies, he would sometimes think of Aaron, and he would wonder whether that was true of him. He had seemed a normal boy, like any of them.

"I'll tell you what has happened to them, this family you knew," Schaefer said. "If they were treated like the others, they were pulled out of the ghetto. They were forced into trains—men and women and children, young and old—and they were shipped to death camps."

"This is all a lie. You've accepted the lies of our enemies. I'm telling you, Schaefer, stop now, because I won't listen." He pushed his fingers up under the curve of his helmet, clamped his hands over his ears.

"Hitler is gassing these people, Dieter—and burning their bodies."

Dieter pulled his hands down. "Burning them? What in the world are you talking about?"

"It's done by the SS. The cowards *murder* Jews, then drag their bodies off to ovens and burn them. I have talked to a man who did all these things—a guard who bragged about the number of Jews who could be burned in a day, the thousands and thousands he had put to death."

"He was a liar, then. I have no idea why you want to believe all this." Dieter was sickened by the thought of such a thing, but he knew it couldn't be true. His Hitler Youth leader had told him that lies like this sometimes circulated, but they were senseless. Why would Germans kill people when labor was so much in demand? It wasn't logical. Some people only wanted to make Germans look bad, didn't care about truth.

But Dieter knew there was no use talking to Schaefer. As soon as he had the chance, Dieter would have to report the man, get him off the line.

"Dieter, listen to me. You have to know this—whether you want to or not."

"No. I don't have to hear it. I hate these lies."

"When this war is over, Dieter, all this will come out. I hope, by then, you lie in bed at night and remember this day and those boys you killed. I hope you'll be ashamed to know you fought for Hitler—a little madman."

"Be quiet. That's enough." He grabbed his ears harder this time, began to hum, so he wouldn't be able to hear.

But Schaefer grabbed Dieter's wrists, hard, and jerked his arms down. "I shot at no one today, Dieter. I aimed beneath those boys. I didn't kill a single one of them. But I have killed, killed plenty in Russia, and what I wish is that I had died instead. I'm ready to die anytime."

"You're a coward. You listen to lies, and then you put your comrades in danger by refusing to shoot the enemy. You will be hanged if you make it through this battle. I'll see to it that you are."

But Dieter was only saying words now, and he was struggling to believe them. He needed his Hitler Youth leader. He needed those who knew the whole truth to join with him. It was too hard to take on Schaefer by himself.

"I want you to live, Dieter. I want you to live long enough to be ashamed. It's what you deserve. Maybe you've been duped and misguided, but there's something wrong with German boys like you—*and me*—that we fall for these things. Hitler visits with you in his fancy train, gives you a piece of junk medal, hardly worth a mark or two, and you're willing to die for that. What's wrong with you? Do you have any idea?"

Dieter was sitting with his rifle next to him. He grabbed it and pressed the barrel against Schaefer's chest. "Stop now. Don't say another word. If you do, I'll pull this trigger and blow you apart. I cannot tolerate one more word."

"Pull the trigger, Dieter. It would be a relief to me, and it would give you one more thing to think about the rest of your life."

Dieter knew he needed to kill Schaefer before he tried to corrupt anyone else. So Dieter squeezed the trigger, hard—or tried to—but nothing happened. The message never seemed to leap from his brain to his finger, and he was humiliated when he let the weapon slip back down to the ground.

CHAPTER 15

"Here they come," Sergeant Pappas whispered, but Spence didn't have to be told. He saw the tanks—three in a line again—roll out of the woods. It was early morning, still mostly dark, but the big Tigers looked like giant black beetles, bucking over the snowdrifts, squirming up the hill. Spence could also see tiny creatures in winter whites, working their way out of the trees. What the Germans didn't know was that reinforcements had been brought in overnight—a whole company. The tanks were formidable, but the Americans definitely had the numbers on their side this time, along with the artillery, and they had the high ground.

Spence didn't move. He knew what he had been told: not to shoot until the Germans were well up the hill. The whole idea was to draw them out. Artillery would open up first. What Spence hoped was that those tanks would retreat once the shells started landing. Lieutenant Nowland kept saying that the Germans were getting short on tanks, and they wouldn't leave them out in the open to get worked over. But if they kept coming—and artillery didn't take them out—the only defense the Americans had was a couple of bazookas, and Pappas had told Spence the antitank guns weren't very effective against the big German *Panzer*. Bazookas could sometimes knock off a track and put a tank out of commission, but they could usually only penetrate the armor if a man was willing to put his life on the line and move in close.

"Why are they doing this?" Spence whispered.

Sergeant Pappas was next to him, lying on the ground. "They're getting desperate, I think. Somebody must be telling them they have to break through and take Bastogne, and do it now."

There was something eerie about it. The Germans were walking into a trap, but Spence hated to watch the whole thing: the slow movement of the troops, climbing in a skirmish line, steadily moving up the hill. He wanted to start shooting, drive them back, and then he wanted to return to his foxhole. He always wanted to be in that hole these days. What he knew was that the Germans still had artillery in the area, and he expected it to start opening up at any second.

But the guns didn't fire and the tanks kept coming, the men. And then, behind him, Spence heard the big

American 105s. The first two blasts struck long, over the tops of the tanks, but Spence saw the German soldiers hold up, the tanks stop, and then the next two explosions were right on target. He saw men fly into the air, turn over, their legs spinning over their heads, like acrobats.

By then the German tanks began to fire. But they were backing off, only lofting up a few shells as they retreated. A couple of explosions burst in front of Spence, down the hill a little, and he ducked his head. Then he heard a crash behind him, in the woods. But the shelling didn't last long, and the tanks soon disappeared. What astounded Spence was that the men kept coming. They must have been assuming that the Americans had been riddled the day before and were undermanned. Still, it was amazingly brave, and Spence watched in awe. The 105s kept the heat on, explosions breaking across the long, open field, but the Germans stayed spread out, and few were being hit. They just kept coming, and the American riflemen, the mortar teams, the machine-gun teams, continued to wait. It was all sort of sickening, these men hunched forward, working their way through the deep snow, not yet realizing that two companies, not just the remains of one, were waiting for them.

The Germans were not more than a hundred yards away when the word went down the line: "Fire at will!"

The machine guns began to clatter—like the putt-putt sound of a single-piston motor—and the blast of rifle fire sounded all up and down the line. Spence didn't worry about aiming at a single target. He merely did as trained, fired to an area in front of him, tried to keep a lot of bullets in the air. But the white uniforms were mostly down now, in the snow. They had taken cover, but they were stranded out in the middle of the hill just as the Americans had been the day before. Artillery and mortar rounds were dropping in on them, however, and if they stayed down they would be wiped out. Spence didn't hear the command, but he knew what was happening. The Germans were being told to get up, to retreat, to get off the hill. He saw them rising like ghosts, turning, trying to get moving in the deep snow. And he saw them falling, saw blood spatter from their uniforms.

But amazingly, some were not hit—more than Spence could imagine. They charged down the hill, falling, tumbling into the snow, rolling and getting up, fighting ahead. Some of them stayed down, but others managed to keep scrambling ahead, and gradually they were blending into the shadows, the white of the snow. In time, some of them disappeared into the trees. But three-fourths of them, maybe more, had stayed down, were out there dead or wounded. Spence had never seen anything like it. He kept thinking of the day before, when he had been the one trying to get away, and he felt a strange identification with the soldiers who were lying in the snow.

The artillery had stopped now, the small-arms fire,

and the silence was strangely unnerving. Spence was breathing harder than he needed to, and the steam kept puffing into the cold, past his eyes. He lay on his stomach, his rifle still ready, but the only soldiers he could see were lumps of white, like mounds in the snow. There were craters, blotches of black earth, but the only color was a spot of red, here and there. A few of the lumps were moving—not getting up, but squirming, perhaps digging bandages from a pack, or maybe just writhing in pain.

Spence heard a few of the Americans laughing, bragging, but most were as silent as Spence. "Just sit tight for right now," Pappas said. "I'm going to see what Nowland wants to do." He got up, stood straight, and walked away.

Spence kept watching the Germans who were down, and he wondered what they were going through. He knew what he feared more than anything—knew what other soldiers said, too—that they didn't want to die slow, all torn up and mutilated. He had to believe that German soldiers felt the same way. Those guys had walked up that hill, brave as anyone could expect, and some of them were in agony now, with no one to help them. Spence didn't want to think about Ted, but he had to wonder, had he really died in an instant, the way Slocum had said, or did he feel that bullet tear through his back and chest, then feel the life drain out of him?

"Can't we send medics down there?" Spence asked, not exactly sure who would answer him.

The soldier next to him, a corporal named Atkins, no more experienced than Spence, said, "I guess they send out their own. It's not our job."

That was probably right, but nothing was happening. People were dying who didn't have to, it seemed, or flopping around in pain like those rabbits Spence had killed, back home. Spence glanced around, wondered what the other men were thinking. He saw Sergeant Pappas, over by Nowland, both of them looking through field glasses. He got up and walked to them, and as he approached, he heard Pappas say, "There's more of them down there than you realize. A lot of them are alive, too. I can see the steam in the air when they breathe."

"Why don't their medics come?" Spence asked.

"I don't know."

"That's not our problem," Nowland said, and he walked away.

"Let me look through your glasses," Spence said.

Pappas continued to watch for a time, but finally he handed the glasses to him. Spence adjusted them a little, and then he scanned the hillside. He saw one of the Germans moving, seeming to be busy at something, probably trying to patch himself up.

And then, for just a moment, the soldier glanced up the hill, toward Spence, and Spence got a good look at his face. He was young—really young. "One of those guys is just a young boy," he said. But it occurred to Spence that the guy probably wasn't a whole lot younger than himself, maybe a year or two. Still, he was one of the farthest up the hill, only 200 yards or so away. He had made a brave charge into all that fire.

"The medics are coming now," someone said, and Spence moved his glasses, spotting the guys with red crosses on their helmets, moving up the hill. One of them kept trudging through the snow, ahead of the others. He eventually reached the boy Spence had seen through the glasses and knelt down next to him.

And then bullets zinged through the air. The medic humped, the way Spence remembered deer doing, when they were standing still and took a bullet. The medic held for a moment, and then slumped to the ground. Spence couldn't believe it. He jumped up and spun to his right. "Hey, what are you doing?" he shouted at a boy—a kid maybe his age, a guy from the other company.

"I just got my first German," the kid said, and he laughed.

"That was a medic."

"We're going to have to kill 'em all before we're finished. I don't care what his job is."

Sergeant Pappas had gotten up. He spoke almost matter-of-factly. "Hey, don't shoot their medics. That ain't right." But there was no passion in his voice, and the soldier didn't respond. A few seconds later, Spence heard him laugh and make some joke to the guy next to him.

One of the men said something about going souvenir hunting down on the hill, once the medics had pulled out.

Spence raised the field glasses again and focused in on the soldier who was down, the one next to the medic. The boy was pulling something from the medic's pack. He probably wanted to bandage himself and stop his own bleeding. He was also yelling for help. When Spence listened closely, he could hear him. But the other medics—three of them—were retreating off the hill, obviously frightened by the gunfire that had taken one of their team.

CHAPTER 16

Spence was sitting in his foxhole, alone. Sergeant Pappas was out checking on the other men. Pappas was a pretty good guy, but he had a lot on his mind. He wasn't one to sit and chat. With time to think now, Spence had Ted on his mind again. He kept wondering about his family. He doubted that a telegram had reached their farm yet, but it wouldn't be long before it did, and Spence knew how devastated the whole family would be. He figured Ted's little brother, Kenny, was going to have the hardest time. A few days before, Ted had let Spence read a letter from the boy. It was simple, with some local news—and lots of misspelled words—but at the end, he had written, "I'm proud of you, Ted. You're fighting for our country, and that's what I want to do, too. Just as soon as they'll let me." Spence hoped that wouldn't happen. He hoped the war would end before Kenny got in on it.

Spence also wondered about his own family, how everyone would feel if something happened to him. He realized now that he hadn't thought enough about that before. He had worried about being brave, being man enough for battle, but he hadn't considered the effect his decision would have on other people. He knew it would be hard for his parents if he were lost, hard, too, for his brothers and sisters, especially for Lloyd. That should have been obvious to him back when he was so eager to join up, but death hadn't been real to him back then. It was something that happened to other people. Now, already, half the guys in his company were dead, either that or all shot up, and he wondered what chance he had of making it through the rest of the war.

As the sun went down, and sounds began to carry across the snow, Spence had noticed a distant sound. It was like the bellowing of a young calf—one that had gotten its leg caught in a barbwire fence. As Spence listened, however, he thought he heard a word. "Shay-fuh," it seemed to be. "Shay-fuh. Shay-fuh." Spence didn't know any German. Maybe that was a way of calling for help.

Sergeant Pappas came back to the foxhole after a time, and Spence asked him whether he had noticed the sound. "Sure, I have," he said. "It sounds like he's saying 'Schaefer.' That's a German name."

On and on, the wailing continued, for maybe two hours. The voice would come, strong the first time, and repeat four or five times, the volume trailing off, and then there would be a long wait, maybe ten minutes, before it came again. After each call, Spence would hear a rasping, wheezing sound as the German sucked for air after the exertion. Each time Spence expected a final gasp, and an end to it. But it would return, seeming as strong as the time before. "Shaayyyy-fuh, Shaayyyy-fuh."

The pain in the boy's voice was pitiful. It hurt Spence, got inside him. And what was worse, he thought he knew which soldier it was. He was almost sure it was that young boy who had been trying to bandage himself—the one the medic had been trying to help when some dumb kid had shot him. The whole idea was sickening. That boy could have been bandaged and then moved off the hill. His agony would have been over. He would have had his ticket home.

"Someone toss a grenade down there and shut that guy up," someone yelled from one of the foxholes. "Put him out of his misery."

That actually did seem a good idea to Spence. The boy was probably bleeding to death and would never make it through the night. It might be better if someone ended everything quickly for the guy. He knew that if he were out there on that hill, in pain, bleeding, maybe freezing, he would want the end to come fast. But that thought only led back to his fears—the ones that had been filling his head. He didn't want everything taken away—all the things he had expected of life. He wanted to see Brigham City again; he wanted to get married, have some little kids who called him "Daddy"; go to work, pay bills; do all the things a man did. There were other girls besides LuAnn. He wanted to find one, wanted to know, once in his life, that some girl loved him, even if he was short, even if he did have crooked teeth.

Maybe tomorrow Spence's company would make another drive, down the hill again, and try to push the Germans back. Sergeant Pappas had said that's what might happen. But if it did, Spence could be the one out there bleeding in the snow. In fact, if they kept making these stupid charges, over and over, how could he possibly hope that his turn wouldn't come? He let that knowledge run around in his head for a while, and then he told himself the truth. All the odds were on the wrong side. And he remembered what Ted had said, that he wished he had never signed up, that he had just stayed home for one more year. Spence thought of Box Elder High, sitting in a warm schoolroom, going to basketball games, eating hamburgers at Dale's.

He shut his eyes and tried to get it all back: home. He pictured Main Street, with the sycamore trees lining the road and hanging over the cars like a canopy. He thought of his house, the way he could look out the kitchen windows toward the Wasatch Mountains and Logan Canyon. He thought of playing basketball with Lloyd, out at the barn, hearing the old wooden backboard rattle when the ball hit the rim. He remembered one morning in the summer, really early, when he had been out working in the orchard with his father, remembered the way the sun had streaked through the trees, and he and his dad had talked about this and that: baseball and boxing and tractors. He wanted another day like that, with his dad. And Mom, with breakfast ready, after his early chores—fried eggs and bacon, hot rolls, butter—humming church hymns while she fussed around in the kitchen.

Sergeant Pappas left again, checked his men, and then, when he came back to the foxhole, all he said was, "It's getting cold." He hunkered down next to Spence.

"That German is still yelling for help," Spence said.

"I know."

"Can't someone help him?"

"Someone ought to kill him."

"Couldn't one of our medics go down and get him?"

"I've seen Krauts shoot our medics rather than accept their help."

That didn't make sense to Spence. It sounded like an excuse. "I'll go down there, if you want. I could maybe patch the guy up and pull him back."

"No, no. If we overrun this hill again tomorrow, our medics will look after him. But they don't go out in front of our lines to help one of their guys."

"But one of our guys shot their medic. That's why the kid is still there."

Pappas hesitated, as though the point carried some weight with him, but then he said, "Maybe so. But we can't do anything about that now."

"He's just a young kid, Sergeant. Really young."

"We can't help that. That's what the Germans are doing now—calling up little boys." And then he laughed. "About like you."

"Shay-fuh!" came the cry again. The voice was getting weaker. "Shay-fuh!"

"If that was some kind of animal, we'd at least go shoot it. There's no way we ought to let that guy moan like that."

"Never mind. There's not one thing we can do. Let's just go to sleep."

But sleep didn't come for Spence, and every time he thought the German was finally dead, the voice would return. It was a moan now, not a desperate cry. It was like a little kid crying after the pain had ended, just crying from momentum, from memory of the hurt. Spence remembered Lloyd, when he was younger, how he would cry like that. But that thought, that connection, was almost too much for Spence. What would he want someone to do, he asked himself, if his own little brother were the one down there?

Sergeant Pappas slept for a time, snored, and Spence thought of trying to climb from the hole without his knowing, but that was impossible. A guy like Pappas slept half awake, ready for trouble. He would surely feel Spence move, and stop him. But eventually the sergeant roused himself. It was late in the night, but he got up and then pulled himself out of the hole. Spence figured that he was going out to check on the outpost, make sure the men out there were all right, hadn't fallen asleep.

Spence had made up his mind by then. If Pappas left, he was going down there. He would crawl to that boy and see what he could do for him. So as soon as Pappas left, Spence stood, and once the sergeant was far enough away, he climbed from the hole.

Spence knew his danger was not from the Germans at this point; it was from his own sentries, who might think he was an infiltrator. So he crawled slowly and quietly down the hill, sometimes waiting for minutes at a time before he moved ahead. It was cold in the snow, and he was scared. He was disobeying orders, taking a huge chance, and he didn't feel right about that, but he had to do this.

As he rested, tried to keep his breathing quiet, he thought of the words again, the ones he heard on Christmas Eve: "How silently, how silently, the wondrous gift is given. So God imparts to human hearts the blessings of his heaven." He had sung those words one year in a Sunday school Christmas pageant. But they hadn't meant this. They hadn't meant much of anything to him. He had heard so many sermons, never considered what he was supposed to do about any of them, but a current of warmth came through him as he sang the rest of the verse in his mind:

"No ear may hear his coming;
But in this world of sin,
Where meek souls will receive him, still,
The dear Christ enters in."

He still wasn't sure what that meant, but he felt like he was doing the right thing, maybe what his dad would have wanted him to do.

He moved ahead, slowly, carefully. At times he lost track of where he was going, but always the sound would return, the call, the heavy breathing. The German was running out of strength, maybe calling out only in his delirium now, not even knowing what he was doing.

Spence took upward of an hour to crawl the distance, and then, as he approached the German, he began to whisper to him. "Don't get jumpy now. I'm coming to help you." And then, between breaths, "Help you. Only help you. I won't hurt you."

"Schay-fuh?" the man whispered, and he sounded distant, as though he were only half awake.

"No. American. But I'll help you."

Spence was frightened as he came close. He didn't want this guy to react, in his confusion, and shoot him.

But the boy was lying on his back, staring upward, and as Spence finally got a look at him, a hint of moonlight on his face, he saw again how young he was. Like Lloyd. Like Kenny.

"I'll help you if I can," he whispered. He got to his knees and looked down on the boy, and the young man's eyes finally seemed to focus. Spence saw the fear, the realization. He threw up his hands, tried to push Spence away.

"I just want to help you," he said, but he could still see the fear in the boy's eyes. And then he thought of the song. "O little town of Bethlehem, how still we see thee lie," he sang. He had no idea whether Germans knew the song, but he watched the frenzy leave the boy's eyes, saw him calm. "Above thy deep and dreamless sleep, the silent stars go by."

There was blood on the boy's pant leg and in the snow. He had wrapped a bandage around the outside of his pants, over the wound, but the bandage wasn't tight, wasn't really doing much good. Spence kept humming the song as he pulled off his gloves and fumbled in his pockets until he found one of the bandages he kept there. He used it to wrap the boy's leg, around the other bandage, and then he pulled it tight, putting pressure on it. If that was the only problem, he could drag the boy partway up the hill, closer to his own lines, and then he could yell for someone to come out and help. At that point, Sergeant

Pappas may not like it, but he couldn't do much about it. He wouldn't stop his men from coming out to help. He might even come down himself.

"Are you hurt anywhere else—or just your leg?"

The boy looked at him with wonder. Clearly, he didn't understand. But when Spence moved around behind his head and gripped him under the arms, he cried out. And Spence saw the problem. He had tugged on the boy's arm just enough to pull his elbow away from his side. He saw where the coat was torn, saw the blood that was seeping from another wound in his ribs. Maybe there was no way to save this kid now. Spence crawled back to his side and lifted his elbow. He didn't know what to do. He had to keep pressure on the wound, and he had to drag him, too. He looked into the boy's eyes, tried to think.

What Spence saw was desperation, dependence. The boy had to know he was dying, know this American offered his only hope. For a moment some clarity seemed to come into his gaze, as though he were seeing Spence as a boy like himself.

Spence thought of the medic's bag. The medic was lying dead, nearby, but his bag was on the snow, open. Spence turned it over, dumped everything out. There were bigger bandages, in rolls. What he couldn't find was any morphine. But he got behind the boy and raised him up. The young man moaned but tried to use some of his own strength to stay seated. Spence placed a big bandage over the outside of his coat, and then rolled a long strip around his entire chest. But it wasn't enough, wasn't tight enough. So Spence unbuckled the belt from his trousers and pulled it loose. Then he wrapped it around the boy's chest and snugged it up, over the bandage, tight enough to make him gasp. "Okay. I'm going to drag you. It's going to hurt. But it's your only chance."

Spence moved back around behind the boy's head, began to hum the song again, reached under him, got hold of him under the arms, and he pulled. The German was heavy in the snow, with his snow uniform dragging, but Spence figured he could move him. Once he cut the distance to his men, he would yell, so they would know what the noise was, but for now, he wanted to move him as far as possible without drawing attention to himself.

Dieter was confused. He wasn't thinking straight. He felt weak, horribly weak. Sometimes, he would drift away, lose touch with what was happening, but then the tug would come under his arms and he would feel the pain through his side, and that would bring him back. What he sensed was that this boy with the kindly voice was helping him. He knew that the soldier was an American, but he didn't seem so. He was just a young man like himself, humming that pretty song, and there was no war in Dieter's head. There was pain, and mostly there was confusion, but there was this boy, too, who had applied new bandages to him, who wanted to pull him off this hill. And sometimes, in this half reality, the boy was Schaefer, his friend Schaefer, looking out for him, finally there to save him.

And then a loud noise shocked Dieter into wakefulness. Someone had fired a rifle. He saw the flash of it, heard the report, from very close. And now a man was over him. A German. "We came for you," he said. "We couldn't stand to hear you yelling all night. We'll get you off this hill."

There were two of them. Two of his comrades. He knew their names, he thought. They were stalwarts, what Germans ought to be. They had come for him after all. They picked him up, the two of them. They lifted him between them, and they tramped down the hill, bouncing and jostling as they went, causing more pain than Dieter could bear, and then after a time, set him down. They breathed hard, and he realized they were resting, but he was not yet back to the camp below. Something was coming clear to him by then. "Where is the American?" he asked.

"We shot him. The swine was trying to take you prisoner. We put him away."

But the American had spoken so quietly, soothingly, had sung to him. He had bandaged Dieter. Had he only wanted to take him in, to question him? Was that it? Dieter couldn't think about that, not with his mind making dreams half the time.

* * *

Spence wanted to yell, but there was no breath in him, no power. He was lying on his back in the snow. And he knew he would die. It was a strange thing to think about, to realize. The pain was filling him up. It had been like fire in his chest at first, and then it had swelled through all of him. Now it was evolving into numbness. But he was still clinging to the wish that all this weren't so. He didn't want to die. He wasn't ready to die.

He kept fighting not to go to sleep. He wanted to yell, to shout for Sergeant Pappas, but he had no voice, no breath, no strength. He tried to look at the sky, the stars, to keep himself awake by staring hard, not give up, but the fight was just too hard. "I'm sorry Dad," he tried to say, and he let his eyes go shut. He thought of the words again, tried to let the words of the song go through his head.

CHAPTER 17

When Dieter awoke, he was inside a tent. He twisted his head to the side and saw that other men were in the cots around him, all of them apparently wounded. This was some sort of field hospital. He tried to remember everything. He had given up a few times, out there on that hill—or was all that a dream? He couldn't think what had happened. How had he gotten here? The pain was back now, the wound in his side only the center place of a vast ache that spread all through him. He tried to shift a little, to see more of what was around him, but the pain gouged him and he knew he couldn't do that. He breathed smoothly several times, and then he asked, "What's going on?"

He didn't know who was there, whom he was asking. But a man next to him, on a cot not a foot away, said, "What do you mean?"

Dieter didn't know what he meant, so he waited, slept a little more, tried to get the confusion out of his head. And at some point he awoke once again, aching, full of fire, and a man was standing over him. A medic. "How did I get here?" Dieter asked.

"I don't know," the man said, and Dieter could hear that he didn't really care. "We've closed you up the best we could. But you need surgery. We're going to move you when we can."

"Will I die?"

"I don't know."

"Did Schaefer bring me here?"

He didn't answer. He was a man with red in his beard, a week's worth of growth. But he had no life left in him, in his eyes. He walked away.

Dieter slept again, and he awakened with Sergeant Franke looking at him. "Hedrick, how are you?" he asked.

Dieter didn't know. He felt strange. When he looked at the sergeant, he knew that something had changed, and he was embarrassed, but he didn't know exactly what the change was, what had happened to him. Then he realized that he wasn't in the war, that he didn't want to be in the war, that he had quit the war out on the hill in the snow. "Where's Schaefer?" he asked.

"Dead."

"On the hill?"

"Yes." Dieter felt this—felt as though he had lost half

his world. He didn't know who cared about him now, could hardly remember his parents. "That's why he didn't come for me," Dieter mumbled, and it seemed as though he had always known that.

"Most of us were hit, Dieter. I took a bullet through my shoulder. That's why I'm here."

Dieter had noticed the sling, but now he saw the change in his sergeant's face.

"It's not so bad, Dieter. We can go home. By the time you're better, the war might be over."

"I'm going to have surgery. A medic told me that."

"I know. But you'll be all right. That's what the doctor told me."

"An American tried to help me."

"What?"

It was the first time Dieter had remembered it, and yet the knowledge had been in his head all while he was trying to wake up. "Out there on the hill. An American came down to me, and he bandaged me. He put his belt around me to hold the bandage tight."

"I don't think so, Dieter. You were hallucinating."

"No. He was young. Like a Hitler Youth boy. But he was an American."

"A medic?"

"No. Just a soldier. But they shot him. I think they killed him."

"Who did?"

"Our soldiers. The ones who came for me. They said the American was taking me prisoner."

"Yes. Of course he was. It was right to kill him."

"No."

"Dieter, many people die in war. You can't think about this all your life."

Dieter tried to think about that. But he knew the truth, and he told it to himself: "I will think about it all my life."

The army wasn't shipping bodies home from Europe. Spence was buried in Belgium. But at home a service was held to honor him. Half the people in Brigham City came. Everyone knew the Morgans.

The Mormon bishop, a dear friend of the family named Heber Stott, opened the meeting, after a prayer, by offering a tribute. "This boy could have stayed home," he said. "He was young enough, and if he had wanted to, he could have stayed around here a little longer. But he believed in the great freedoms we all love in this country. He knew that he had to defend our nation against the Nazis—Satan's warriors. He knew that if he didn't do it, someone else would have to go, so he stepped up and said, 'Let me do my share. Let me face the enemy and show them that they can't spread their evil across this world.' So today we honor this noble young man, who freely gave his life for our freedom. He is a hero, and his name will be remembered in this town forever."

The Morgans sat together, all in a line. Robert was home for the funeral, wearing his navy dress whites. Louise was holding on to Evelyn and Betty, one under each arm. Dad and Mom had Lloyd between them, holding him up. The boy had cried for three days straight.

"Spencer went to war, but he didn't let it corrupt him," the bishop said. "He stayed true to his faith. So there is reason to celebrate today. A young man has met the challenge, has lived righteously and honorably, and will receive his just reward."

LuAnn Crowther was in the congregation, with her fiancé, Dennis Stevens. They spoke to the Morgans after the meeting. "I've talked to Dennis about it," she said. "If we have a son, we want to name him Spencer. He was such a wonderful boy."

Later that day the family gathered out on the Morgan farm. Lots of relatives came. They all talked about Spence, what a good boy he had always been. But his father, after a time, had heard enough. He went to his room, his and his wife's bedroom, and he sat on the bed.

A letter had come from Spence's sergeant, a man named Pappas. Mr. Morgan took it out from his drawer and read the final paragraph again:

I thought you would want to know how your son died. He crawled from our position onto the field of battle. I don't know what happened exactly, but he was hit by enemy fire. He had told me earlier that he wanted to help a wounded boy he had spotted, a German boy, out in the field, and I had ordered him not to do it. But he went, anyway. It's not the sort of thing a soldier gets a medal for, dying for an enemy, but I'll never forget it as long as I live. None of the men will. Spencer was everything you must have hoped he would be. I could always tell what a fine family he came from, the way he lived. I'm just sorry this happened.

The Morgans had thought about reading the letter at the memorial service, but they couldn't bring themselves to do it. With all the talk of war, all the hatred of Japs and Germans, who would understand it? What would people think?

But Mr. Morgan thought of all the promises Spence had kept.

HE WAS WILLING TO FIGHT FOR HIS COUNTRY.
BUT WOULD HIS COUNTRY FIGHT FOR HIM?

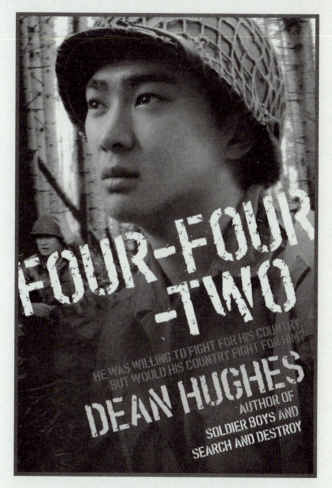

Turn the page to start reading
FOUR-FOUR-TWO,
another thrilling war story from Dean Hughes.

December 1941

Yuki Nakahara was stacking wooden boxes accord-ing to size in a musty storage shed. As he walked past the open door, he saw a car driving up the dirt road toward the farm. It was traveling too fast, jolting, dust billowing up behind it. Yuki stopped and watched. He could see that the car was a new '41 Ford—a fancier car than he usually saw this far away from Berkeley—and Yuki was almost sure he knew what that meant. He felt himself tighten, his chest suddenly rigid, but he had no idea what he should do.

The black car stopped between the storage shed and the house. Two men got out, both of them wearing dark suits and hats. They each turned and looked around, clearly checking out the farm, the buildings. One of the men noticed Yuki, so Yuki stepped from the shed and tried to look calm. He walked toward the tall man on the driver's side. The man removed his hat and asked, "Is your father home, young man?"

Yuki didn't like the look of the guy. His dark hair was combed back slick, and his shirt collar was stiff and bright white—like he was someone official. His voice had sounded polite, but the look in his narrowed eyes was menacing.

"Are you produce buyers, or—"

"We need to talk to your father." The man's tone was suddenly curt, but then he brought it under control as he said, "Would you please take us to him?"

Yuki thought of running to his father, telling him to hide. But he knew he couldn't do that. "I saw him walk into the house a few minutes ago," Yuki said. "I'll see if he's still there." He walked past the man and headed toward the house.

Both men followed, walking fast enough to keep up. The second man—a smaller fellow with a brown suit, black hair, dark eyes—caught up to Yuki at the front door, where Yuki stopped to remove his boots. "Leave your shoes on," the man said. "We'll go in with you. Just tell your father someone wants to see him—nothing else." He had a low, hard voice and some kind of accent, maybe New York. Yuki nodded, but he shoved the door open and stepped hard on the hardwood floor inside. He wanted to make as much noise as possible. The two men separated inside the little living room and stood on either side of him. Yuki thought of shouting to his father, telling him to run out the back door, but Father would never do that. He would be respectful. It was the way he dealt with white people, always.

When Yuki took a step toward the kitchen, the bigger man reached out and grabbed his shoulder, held him back. And then he announced, "Mr. Nakahara, we need to speak to you. We're agents from the Federal Bureau of Investigation."

Yuki's mother stepped into the living room from the kitchen. She was wearing a white apron over her housedress. Her hair was pulled back tight against her head. She was tiny, but now she took a breath and raised her shoulders. She looked directly at the men—one and then the other. "I'm Mrs. Nakahara. What may I do for you?" she asked.

The man removed his hat. "Is Mr. Nakahara at home?" he asked.

"Is there anything I can—"

"My name is Agent Carson. This is Agent Aldo. As I said, we're from the FBI. We need to speak to your husband." Now there was more force in his voice.

Father had appeared by then, behind Mother. He was wearing his work clothes, a bulky wool jacket over overalls. He had taken off his boots, and in his stocking feet, he seemed to shrink before the men.

"Are you Mr. Nakahara?"

Father nodded, or maybe bowed just slightly.

"Do you publish a Japanese-language newspaper?"

He nodded again.

"We understand you keep close ties to people in Japan. Is that right?"

Mother said, "He doesn't speak much English, Mr. Carson. He has relatives in Japan, and he writes letters to them now and then, but his ties are all to this country now. He has lived here for more than thirty years."

"Well, that's what *you* say," Agent Aldo said. "But he's on our list. Tell him we're arresting him."

Yuki's breath stopped.

Father spoke better English than Mother was letting on, and he had surely understood the word "arrest," but he didn't move, didn't show any reaction.

Mother's hands had jumped, as though of their own accord, but then she grasped them together. Yuki saw her blink, knew she was fighting tears, but her voice was strong when she said, "I don't understand. What are the charges against my husband?"

"I told you, he's on a list. Tell him he's got to come with us."

"But you can't arrest him for no reason. He hasn't done anything wrong." She took a step sideways, placing herself in front of her husband.

"If that's the case, he has nothing to worry about,"

Agent Carson said. "But for right now, he has to come with us."

"Where will you take him?"

"I'm sorry, ma'am, it's not our job to explain everything to you. We've been sent to bring him in. I guess you'll hear from others who can tell you the details."

"Must he go with you right now? Can't he—"

"I'm afraid we're going to take him now. We do need to search your house, however. I want you and your son to sit right here in the living room while we put your husband in our car. Then one of us will come back and do the search."

"Search for what?"

"Look, lady," Aldo said, "you don't ask the questions. We do. Sit down, you and your son. Do you have other children?"

"Yes. Two daughters and another son."

"Where are they?"

"Not home from school yet. They come on a bus."

"And what about you?" He looked at Yuki. "Don't you go to school?"

"I get out earlier, so I help my father on the farm. We work hard. We're *Americans*. We—"

"Stop right there. I don't want to hear all that," Aldo said.

Carson put up his hand, as if to say "That's enough" to his partner. "We're going to ask you to go with us now, Mr. Nakahara," he said.

"I must change clothes," Father said.

"No, sir, you don't need to do that. They'll have clothes for you where you're going. Were those your shoes on the porch?"

"Yes."

"Just grab them as we go out. That's all you'll need."

Agent Aldo stepped forward and took hold of Mr. Nakahara's arm. "Come with us now," he said. He pulled on Father's elbow and Father stumbled forward, then caught his balance and looked at Mother. "Where am I going?" he asked in Japanese. Yuki had attended Japanese language school when he was younger. He didn't speak Japanese fluently, but he understood most things his parents said.

Mother didn't answer her husband. She stepped toward Carson. "You can't do this. This is America. You must tell us what he is charged with."

"You speak English very well," Carson said in an almost friendly tone. "How long have you lived in our country?"

"Most of my life. It's my country too."

"You're an enemy alien, ma'am. Not a citizen."

"My children are citizens. How can you take their father from them?"

"We don't get into all that. We just—"

"I learned about American laws in school. You must tell my husband which law he's broken. You cannot take him away without doing that."

"Actually, in time of war, in a war zone, under direction of our government, we can arrest those who may be a danger to others. This area has been designated a war zone by the government, and your husband has been listed as a probable spy. We don't have to tell you all that, but now we have. Please get out of our way and let us do our job." He took hold of Father's other arm, at the elbow, and the two men led him toward the door, Father not resisting.

"You must not do this," Mother was saying, her voice now desperate. She rushed ahead, got between the men and the front door. "My husband is not a danger to anyone. Can't you see that?"

Aldo turned suddenly and stepped close to Mother. "That's enough, lady. Your husband's a sneaky little slant-eyed *Jap*. That's all we need to know." He glared into her eyes, as if to see how she might react, but Mrs. Nakahara's face only hardened. "On Sunday a bunch of sneaky slant-eyed Japs—just like him—bombed our country. His crime is, he's on their side, not ours. And we're not going to let him make contact with his buddies who are waging a war against us. Now, get out of our way or I'll take you in with him." He used his forearm to sweep her aside.

Yuki had watched all this, not knowing what to do or say, but he finally reacted. As the men took Father out the door, he followed, and then he hurried in front of Agent Carson and stood his ground. "Listen, sir, we run a business here. We grow fruits and vegetables and sell them at a stand down on the highway. I think you've gotten the wrong idea about us somehow. Is there someone we could talk to? I think this could all be straightened out in a few minutes. My father has a little newspaper that he sends out to the old-timers from Japan around here, but that's all it is. He doesn't bother anyone at all. He's no troublemaker."

It was Aldo who answered. "Oh, I see. I'm glad you cleared that up for us. But you know what? You're a sneaky little slant-eyed Jap yourself, and I don't trust you any more than your traitor of a dad. Now, shut your mouth and go back in the house."

"But there's no need for this, sir. Isn't there someone I can talk to?"

"Yeah. Talk to Mr. Hirohito, the emperor of Japan. See what he can do for you. Now, get out of my way."

Yuki's anger suddenly fired. "You can't treat us like this!" he yelled into Aldo's face.

Aldo slammed both hands into Yuki's chest, sent him stumbling backward. In his rage, Yuki was about to charge the man, but he heard his father's voice, not loud, but firm. "No!"

Yuki stopped at the command, but mostly because he knew that he was only making things worse.

"Shikata ga nai," Father said.

Yuki hated that idea, "it can't be helped." It was

something his father believed and often said. It was the Japanese way of thinking—the old way. Yuki was too American for such acceptance. And yet, there really was nothing he could do. He stepped aside.

Carson grabbed Father's boots, and the two men pushed past Yuki, then opened the car door and forced Father into the backseat. Aldo stayed outside by the car, apparently to make sure that Father didn't try to make a run for it. Carson returned to the house, and he systematically worked his way through the five rooms while Yuki sat with his mother, his arm around her shoulders. All that strength she had tried to show was gone now and she was weeping, her hands over her face.

"I knew this was coming," Yuki said. "All Father thinks about is Japan. I told him to burn all the Japanese stuff he has around the house, but he wouldn't do it."

"How could he do that?"

"The same way a lot of people have been doing."

Yuki had talked to his friend Shigeo Omura about the things happening in California these last few days, since Japan had bombed Pearl Harbor and war had been declared. At lunch on Tuesday, Shig had whispered to him, "They're rounding up anyone who's considered a community leader. Your dad's known—because of his newspaper. He's got to throw out that Buddhist shrine he keeps in your house. My parents have gotten rid of everything in our house that looks Japanese."

Yuki had told his father what he needed to do, but Father had said nothing, done nothing. It was always his way. A son didn't tell a father what to do.

"My father's not like yours," Yuki had told Shig. But he decided not to explain what he meant by that. Instead, he asked, "How are kids treating you?"

Yuki and Shig had carried their lunches to school in paper bags. When Yuki was younger, his mother had prepared him a Japanese bento box, with rice and fish, but kids had turned up their noses at the smell. In high school, he and Shig had switched to bologna sandwiches and apples, like everyone else. But this week, since the attack on Pearl Harbor, they had sat in a corner of the lunchroom, at the end of a table, away from others.

"They stare at me," Shig said. "No one's ever paid any attention to me before, and they're not saying anything to me now, but all week, I've seen them looking at me—like I'm not the guy I was before."

Yuki nodded. "It's been the same for me," he said. "Some boy I don't even know said I should 'go back to Japan'—like I've ever been there. But he didn't say it to my face. He whispered it behind me in the hallway and then he slipped into the crowd so he didn't have to look me in the eye."

Two girls approached the table with their lunches, but they stopped short and turned away, leaving the table mostly empty in the crowded lunchroom. Yuki thought of welcoming them, but he knew that although it would have been all right the week before, it wasn't now.

"People *like* you, Yuki," Shig said. "You're popular. They'll get over the shock before long, and they'll know you haven't changed. But me, I'm just the little shrimp I've always been. The war only makes things worse."

"Hey, you're the best second baseman this school's ever had. The guys who play with us know that."

"That doesn't matter anymore."

Yuki and Shig had played baseball together for many years. Yuki had always played shortstop and Shig second base, and they had become a great double-play combination. It was true that Shig was really small—only about five feet tall—and he was quiet, so maybe that was why people didn't notice him around the school. The ball-players had always teased him about having no strike zone and about wearing glasses. But Shig was smart, and when he let loose a little, he was funny. He let Yuki get all the attention and do most of the talking, but when Yuki was struggling, especially with his stern father, Shig would always listen.

What Yuki also knew was that he was going to need Shig more than ever now that the white kids were turning away from them. He had always considered himself friends with people of all races. He had played sports, gone to dances, hung out at soda fountains, and girls had liked to dance with him because he did the jitterbug so well. He had bought himself an old jalopy of a car and had taken girlfriends to the movies, worn the latest styles, been a regular guy. Now—overnight—he was "the enemy."

The lunchroom was full of noise, the same as ever. Maybe a war had started, but kids were talking and laughing the way they always had. But now Yuki could see three Japanese American girls he knew headed for the table where he and Shig were sitting. This was becoming an island for the Japanese students, and yet, that was the last thing any of them wanted.

"Will you stick with me, Yuki?" Shig asked.

Yuki was taking a drink from his Coke bottle. He put it down. "What do you mean, Shig? Of course I'll—"

"It's going to be tougher now. This war might last a long time. If people are going to stare at me all day, every day, I'm going to go crazy. I need someone I can be 'normal' around."

"Hey, I need the same thing. We'll look out for each other."

But now, at home, with the arrest of Yuki's father, things had taken a new turn. It struck Yuki that he was going to have to provide for his family. Maybe he would have to drop out of school. He glanced at his mother, saw how devastated she was. "Don't worry," he told her. "We'll be all right. I'll keep the farm going." But Yuki knew the truth: *Everything* had changed, and nothing was going to be easy.

Agent Carson carried out a lot of stuff: copies of the newspaper Father published, a ceremonial sword that Father had brought with him from Japan, some paper lanterns, a set of binoculars and a flashlight, some letters written in Japanese, and even the Buddha statue from Father's shrine. Then, for some reason, Carson came back and got the tabletop radio that sat on a kitchen shelf. "Why take our radio?" Mother asked, but Carson didn't answer.

"I didn't find any guns. Are there any on your property? Maybe out in that shed?"

"We don't own guns," Mrs. Nakahara said. "We have no need for them."

"I'll just say this: You better not be lying. If you're caught with weapons at any time, your husband won't be the only one locked up." He touched the brim of his hat. "We'll be going now. Be sure to follow the new curfew laws—don't go out after eight o'clock in the evening. I'm sure you'll hear from your husband at some point. Thank you for your cooperation." With the radio under his arm, he walked out to the car.

Yuki got up and watched. He could see his father hunched in the backseat, staring ahead. The agents drove away, the car once again raising a plume of dust. Mother stood up, came to Yuki. He took her in his arms and she sobbed against his shoulder. "There must be someone I can talk to," Yuki said. "We have to get this straightened out."

"No one will listen to us, Yuki. You know that."

But Yuki didn't want to believe it. He was an American, a citizen, and his family was loyal to the United States. They were farmers, churchgoers; they operated a produce business and paid their taxes. Father may have kept his shrine and he may have retained his love for Japan, but he was grateful for all he had been able to achieve here. And Mother was a "church lady," a Methodist, who spoke English more correctly than most, with no Japanese accent at all. What more could people expect of them?

April 1943

Yuki held Keiko's hand as they walked from the
dance floor. The dining hall where the teen dances were
held on Friday nights was much too warm, and Yuki had
been trying out all his jitterbug steps, so sweat was bead-
ing up on his forehead and his shirt was sticking to his
back. But Keiko looked pleased with herself, and Yuki had
the feeling that she was pleased with him, too. She was
two years younger than he was, and she had always been
"Shig's little sister" to him—but she had grown up a lot in
the last year, and recently it had struck him that she was
probably the cutest girl in the whole camp.

Yuki spotted Shig standing by the wall. There was a
big crowd tonight, and there were plenty of girls to dance
with, but so far Shig hadn't asked any of them. That was
nothing new. Shig just wasn't confident in his dancing,

and especially in his ability to talk with girls. In spite of all the changes in their lives—the roundup of Japanese Americans on the coast, and the transport to this desert camp in Utah—Shig was pretty much the same kid he had always been.

"Hey," Shig said, "you two can *swing* it. I didn't know you had it in you, Keiko."

Keiko smiled, showing her dimples—which Yuki loved to look at. She had an innocent, round face and quick eyes. And her skin, flushed a little now, was delicate, perfect. "I've been practicing with my girlfriends," she said, "but Yuki knows more tricks. Did you see him throw me in the air?" She raised her arms to imitate the way he had lifted her.

"Hey, *everyone* saw him do that," Shig said. "You better be careful, little girl—and keep your dress down."

That obviously embarrassed Keiko. She slapped Shig across his shoulder and walked away.

"Don't give her a hard time," Yuki told Shig.

"I'm not. I was just teasing her. But what's going on with you two? Do you like my little sister?"

"Hey, she's cute as a bug's ear. What's not to like?" The truth was, Yuki liked her a lot more than he wanted to admit. He had flirted with her at lunch one day, and the joking had evolved into a long conversation. Since then, they had talked almost every day. What he had realized was that she was not only cute, but smart, and surprisingly thoughtful about life. A lot of Japanese girls thought they had to be quiet and deferential around men—the way their mothers were—but Keiko wasn't afraid to express her opinions and even disagree with Yuki at times.

"Yuki, she's only sixteen."

"I know. But you know what? When I get back from the war, she's going to be all grown up. And who knows, maybe I'll grow up myself." He put his hands on Shig's shoulders and pretended to be serious. "The way I see it, your family would be *greatly* honored if I married her. By then, I'll be better looking than ever—if that's even possible—and I'll have about fifty medals on my chest."

"Or maybe a bullet hole between your eyes."

"Not me. I'm quick as a jackrabbit. No one's going to shoot me." He made a little sideways jump and ducked his head.

The music had started again—the Mills Brothers singing "Glow Worm." It was just a record in a jukebox, but it was loud in the low-ceilinged building. The dancers were all Japanese American, but the "American" part was the obvious part. Most of the girls were wearing bobby socks and saddle oxfords or penny loafers, and cute cotton print dresses or stylish skirts and blouses. The guys had arrived in sports jackets and ties, but most had set their coats aside by now.

"Come here a second, Yuki," Shig said. He walked to the nearby entrance and stepped out into the night air. It was April, and lately the days had been warm in the high-elevation Utah desert, but nights were still cold. That cool air felt good to Yuki as he stepped outside. "Have you made up your mind for sure?" Shig asked. "Are you really going to enlist?"

"You know I am. And so are you."

"Maybe. I'm still not sure."

"You've got to go with me, Shig. You can't break up the ol' double-play combination."

But Yuki had sounded a little too serious, even to himself. He looked up at the stars in the darkening sky. As much as he tried to hide it, he had a hard time fighting back his fear of leaving his mother, going off to war. Japanese Americans were not being drafted into the military like everyone else, but they were now being recruited, and some were choosing to sign up. For most of the guys in camp, it was not an easy decision.

Yuki and Shig now lived in the Central Utah Relocation Center, known as Topaz. After Yuki's father had been arrested during those final days of 1941, the Nakaharas had received no word from him for quite some time. He finally wrote that he had been hauled off to a prison in Montana. He still hadn't been charged with a crime, but he offered no hope that he would return before the end of the war. From then on, Yuki had felt the full weight of responsibility for his family, of making sure that they at least had food on their table.

Then, in March 1942, Yuki had seen a man pasting a sheet of paper on a telephone pole in downtown Berkeley. He had an idea what the sign might say, but he still felt a stab of pain when he read the words. Executive Order 9066 had been passed by Congress and signed into law by President Roosevelt. All Japanese who lived in the West Coast states—whether citizens or not—were required to register with the government. What followed in April was worse. With only a few days' warning, more than 110,000 AJA—Americans of Japanese ancestry—were commanded to assemble at various sites for "relocation." The order stated that they should bring only what they could carry, which meant one or two suitcases and the clothes they were wearing.

Mother, and especially Yuki's sisters, May and Kay, had been devastated. His brother, Mick, had been silent but clearly resentful. Lots of rumors were going around by then, but no one knew where this relocation would take them. All Yuki knew was that he had to hold things together, act confident whether he was or not, and offer his family what consolation he could think of.

The Nakaharas' farm was only leased, since *Issei*—first-generation Japanese immigrants—were not allowed to own land. Still, the tractor, truck, and equipment couldn't just sit on a farm that the family would no longer occupy. Everything had to be sold immediately. Father had left a little money in a bank, but Japanese accounts had been frozen by the government and Mother couldn't access any of her own money. Yuki was baffled that such a thing could happen in the "land of the free."

The morning after seeing the posted order, Yuki had picked up the *Oakland Tribune* and read the headline JAPS GIVEN EVACUATION ORDERS HERE. The term "Jap" was not new, but it had always been considered disrespectful. Now it was being printed in the newspapers.

Throughout the spring, Yuki had tried to manage the farm and still go to school every day. His mother wouldn't hear of him dropping out. He had to be the one to accept forty dollars for a tractor that was worth three hundred, and courteously thank the man who had started out by offering thirty. A lot of their other things—furniture, kitchen items, books—had to be stacked in a barn loft, and there was no telling what would happen to any of it. Mrs. Nakahara was furious, but she told her children as they prepared to leave their house, "Dress in your Sunday clothes, and hold your heads up. The government is shaming itself, but we never will."

Yuki lived with a barely controlled anger, but he kept thinking ahead. When the war was over, he had to be ready to make a life for himself and for his family. It was obvious to him that he had to avoid all appearance of being anything but a loyal American.

At first, Yuki's family, along with Shig's, had been housed in stinking, fly-infested horse stables at the

Tanforan Racetrack in San Bruno, south of San Francisco. Then, after a few months of that humiliation, they had been transported by train to Utah, where barracks covered only in tar paper had been quickly thrown together. Each barracks was divided into six small rooms. The Nakaharas had to squeeze into primitive quarters, twelve feet wide and twenty feet long, with no partitions. Most mortifying were the public toilets. In each was a long board with holes cut in it, and no dividers in between. Yuki's sisters would sometimes wait most of the day to find a moment when they could sneak into the women's side alone.

The desert of central Utah was fiercely hot in the summer, and then the "internees"—just a nice word for "prisoners," as far as Yuki was concerned—survived suffocating dust storms in the fall. The constant wind blew right through the loosely constructed walls and floors. Winter on the high plateau was brutal, with no insulation in the walls and only a small coal stove for heat—and coal in short supply. Yuki and his family tried to make the best of their situation by building furniture from boxes and waste lumber and by planting a garden in the alkaline soil, but nothing felt normal. Most everyone housed in the camp had lived all their lives in the lush San Francisco Bay area. Now they were stuck in this remote place, on ugly, arid land. The nearest town, Delta, was fifteen miles away, and around the camp was nothing but sagebrush and greasewood. To Yuki, it looked like a broad stretch of nothingness.

Schools had been established in the camp by fall, and now, in the spring of 1943, Yuki was about to complete his senior year of high school. Teachers had been recruited from the area, and a few had been excellent, but others had hardly known their subjects. What discouraged Yuki most, however, was knowing that going on to college would have little or no value, since most AJA would not be able to get jobs in the careers they chose. Who was going to hire a Japanese teacher or engineer?

And yet, in spite of all that, the young men were now being recruited to enlist as soldiers—to fight for America. During the winter, Yuki and Shig had both turned eighteen, so they knew they would have to make a choice. For many of the men in the camp, the idea of defending the same country that had taken away their freedom was unthinkable. *Nisei*—second-generation Japanese Americans—supposedly possessed full citizenship, but they found themselves surrounded by tall barbed-wire fences and guard towers. Everyone in camp knew the story of the older man who had wandered out toward the fence one day and been shot and killed by a guard. The guard claimed that the man had been trying to crawl under the fence—but the bullet had struck him in the chest. He had obviously been standing up, facing the guard. And the question was, where could he have gone anyway? Out into the desert? Government spokesmen liked to say that the AJA were being kept in camps for their own safety, but if that were the case, the people asked, why were the machine guns in the guard towers pointed inward, not outward?

Standing outside now, Yuki lowered his gaze from the stars to the distant mountains—just a hint of a purple silhouette against an almost dark sky. Lately he had felt as though he were hanging over a cliff, his fingerhold slipping away. "Shig, we have to join up," he said. "It's the only way we'll ever be respected in this country."

"I'm not sure it will make any difference."

"You've listened to too many of those 'no, no' guys. But look what's happened to them."

Earlier in the year, a controversy had broken out at Topaz and the other camps. The War Relocation Authority had made an attempt to discover how many of the interned people were willing to proclaim their loyalty to America. Imprisoning people based only on their race was not easy to justify, and government officials were looking for a way to release some of the internees and avoid the expense of housing and feeding them. The questionnaire, however, asked two questions that bothered many AJA. Question 27 asked those of draft age whether they would be willing to serve in the military, and question 28 asked whether they were willing to swear allegiance to the United States and forswear allegiance to Japan. Yuki was shocked when he read the second question. He was an American citizen. Why should he have to swear off allegiance to a foreign country? All the same, he wrote "yes" to both questions, knowing that a "no" would give the wrong impression.

As it turned out, those who had written "no" to the two questions were labeled "disloyals" and transferred to a camp in the California desert where they would be carefully watched and segregated from "loyals." This way of handling things had created bitterness even in those who had answered "yes" or who had left the questions blank, and Yuki knew that Shig had struggled when one of their good friends—who certainly was no danger to anyone— had been hauled away.

"I know how you feel about Kenji," Yuki continued. "I feel the same way. But—"

"It's not just that. And I'm not a chicken. But I'm not sure I want to die for people who hate my guts."

"We won't die. We'll come home war heroes, and those same people will be thanking us."

"I doubt that. You know what people called us when we worked in the beet fields."

Yuki and Shig and a lot of others had been allowed to go off camp to help harvest sugar beets—and they had worked hard. But several times, people had driven past the farm and yelled, "Filthy Japs!" And when Yuki and Shig had tried to go to a movie, the manager—a pudgy young guy who looked about the right age to be serving in the army himself—had stood at the door and said, "We don't allow Japs in here, so move on."

Yuki had laughed and said, "Listen, friend, we're from California. We're Americans, just like you. I'm a Methodist, for crying out loud. A Boy Scout."

The young fellow had looked surprised for a moment, as though he hadn't expected Yuki to sound like other teenagers. "Well, people still don't want to sit next to you in a dark theater," he said, but he sounded less adamant than he had at first.

"What do they think? That we're going to sneak up and cut their throats?" Yuki bent over and pretended to draw a knife across someone's neck. "Hey, we're out there digging sugar beets—for the war effort—and we love America, the same as you. I'm going to join the army as soon as they'll let me."

The guy seemed disarmed by that. He stared at Yuki for a time, and then he merely said, "Well, anyway, I can't let you in. That's what the owner told me."

"That's all right. We understand. We're not trouble-makers."

The man had nodded, actually seemed halfway friendly, and Yuki had felt good about the conversation. It was what he had been doing for years. When he had worked at his father's produce stand, he had always been able to tell when shoppers were hesitant to deal with a Japanese clerk, so Yuki had learned to go out of his way to be helpful, to chat with people about the weather, or about sports—which he knew as well as anyone—and he almost always felt that he broke through with people. Some became steady customers and would laugh and talk with him whenever they came in.

But Shig had never possessed Yuki's ease with people. When he had played baseball, the chatter started when he came to bat. Players on opposing teams called him "shrimp," and "four eyes," and sometimes, behind his back, "that little Jap." Yuki had always taken any abuse or teasing he had faced and had been able to toss it back at the white guys, but Shig had never been able to do that.

"I'll tell you what else makes me mad," Shig continued. "They're making up a whole regiment of *Nisei* soldiers. White guys refuse to fight alongside us."

"I know. But it's not so strange if guys like to be around their own people. I hate this camp, but it's kind of nice to be on our own, where we all understand each other. The trouble is, sooner or later we have to get past all that stuff—and just not think about what race we are. For now, though, the way I look at it, if we're the best regiment in the whole army, we'll *demand* respect—and we'll get it."

"And what makes you so sure we're going to be that good?"

Yuki had to think about that. He tucked his hands in his pockets. He didn't like the desert, but he did love the amazing smear of stars across the night sky, and that's what he looked at now.

"Shig," he said, after a time, "I'll tell you how I feel about giving my all to this war." But he hesitated, still a little unsure he could say the words. "I keep saying that the government had no right to put my father in prison. And that's true. He's not a spy, and he's not a traitor. But there's something I've always known about him. He's not an American the way my mother is, and he never will be. His heart has always stayed with Japan. I don't want to be like that. If I want to be respected, I have to give over my loyalty to *this* country, entirely. The white guys are signing up and going out to risk their lives to protect America. If I don't enlist, I'm the same as my father—Japanese at heart."

Shig didn't speak for a while. Yuki knew that Shig's father was much more American in his thinking. He was a farmer, but he raised flowers and marketed them as a wholesaler. He dealt with businesses all through the West. He had no thoughts of returning to Japan. Shig didn't have to feel ashamed of him.

Finally Shig said, "I know what you're saying. I'm an American and I want to do my part. But would we be 'protecting' America? The Japanese navy is already retreating. They'll never drop bombs on the mainland, and how's Hitler supposed to attack us over here?"

"Shig, the Nazis could still take over all of Europe, and

then what happens to our world? Hitler is rounding up Jews and—"

"And putting them in camps. How's that worse than what our country is doing to us?"

It was the question a lot of young Japanese American men were asking.

"I just like to believe that Americans will think this all over sooner or later, and finally get it right. But that will never happen under a dictator like Hitler. He'll never stop until someone stops him, and he thinks that anyone who isn't blond and blue-eyed is worthless. If Germany controls the world, what kind of world will it be?"

Shig nodded but didn't say anything.

"Am I right?"

"Yeah. I think so. But I still have to make up my own mind."

Yuki had been too serious for too long. He didn't want to argue with Shig. "I'll tell you why *I* am going to be a great soldier," he said. "I'll fight the way I dance—smooth but *snappy*." Yuki grinned and gave Shig a little punch in the shoulder, and then he began his jitterbug steps, even pretended to swing a girl under his arm. "You're sure going to be embarrassed if I'm your brother-in-law and a big-shot war hero and you have to admit that you spent the war sitting here in this dumpy camp."

"Hey, stay away from Keiko. I don't want to be related to you." But Shig was finally laughing.

"You have to enlist, Shig. We're a team. Quit thinking so much. Let's go see what the world looks like—and shoot a few Nazis while we're at it."

"Papa says I need to graduate from high school first."

"Don't worry about that. I talked to the camp director. He said we're close enough. He'll let us have our diplomas right now. So what other excuses do you have?"

Shig hesitated, and then he said, "I want to go, Yuki. But I do need to talk to my parents one more time."

"Okay. But you're eighteen. You don't need their permission."

"I know. But I want it."

Yuki nodded. That was something he did understand. But he was enlisting—in spite of what his mother had been telling him.

Yuki pointed to the door. "For now, let's give some girls the chance to dance with us. It's what they're dreaming about in there, and we can't let them down."

Yuki was still laughing when he reached for the door handle, but then he stopped. He joked too much sometimes and he knew it. There was something Shig needed to know. He turned back and said, "I need you, buddy. We promised to stick together forever. I feel like I've got to enlist, but I just can't do it without you."

Shig nodded. "I know," he said. "I feel the same way."

Stone Mirrors
The Sculpture and Silence of Edmonia Lewis

Jeannine Atkins

A GORGEOUS, HAUNTING BIOGRAPHICAL VERSE NOVEL
OF A HALF NATIVE AMERICAN, HALF AFRICAN
AMERICAN SCULPTOR WORKING IN THE YEARS
RIGHT AFTER THE CIVIL WAR.

✱ "A memorable, poetic tale that offers a fictional account of what life
may have been like for Edmonia. . . . A fascinating, tantalizing glimpse."
—*Kirkus Reviews*, starred review

✱ "Splendid. . . . How this brave, driven young woman overcame
prejudice and trauma to pursue her artistic calling to the highest level . . .
is a story that warrants such artful retelling."
—*Booklist*, starred review

"Written with sensitivity and grace, this compelling title of injustice
and vindication will leave readers pondering the complicated
relationship between pain and art."
—*Bulletin of the Center for Children's Books*

FROM atheneum PRINT AND EBOOK EDITIONS AVAILABLE Visit us at simonandschuster.com/teen

WHERE THINGS COME BACK

JOHN COREY WHALEY

"EVERY NOW AND THEN A BOOK RISES TO THE TOP. THIS ONE SOARS."
—ELLEN HOPKINS, BEST-SELLING AUTHOR, CRANK TRILOGY

★"In this darkly humorous debut, Whaley weaves two stories into a taut and well-constructed thriller. . . . Whaley gradually brings the story's many threads together in a disturbing, heartbreaking finale that retains a touch of hope."
—**Publishers Weekly**, starred review